HOLLYWOOD HUSH

ROCHELLE ANNETTE

Interior design by Mitch Green of Rad Press Publishing

Dedicated to Adoptees, Abuse Survivors, and Spiritual
Warriors for Truth. We are the bridge of light, enlightening
consciousness through higher vibrational frequencies.
It's time to rise. The truth will set us free.

I LOVE YOU

I love you because, we are truly one,
I see your true self, shining brighter than the sun,

My love is laced, with compassion when you fall,
I too know that fear, of remembering our souls call,

Every soul is perfect, in the higher realms it's true,
Living here on earth a test, of bringing you back to the real you,

Nothing more I say, will make sense until you know,
The love I have, is the love you have, and we are one in the afterglow.

HOLLYWOOD HUSH
ROCHELLE ANNETTE

CHAPTER ONE

It was mid March, 2007. After a long night performing a stake-out for a client, Ron finally made it home. He threw his briefcase and digital camera onto the desk and headed up the stairs to his bedroom. As he headed towards his room, Ron paused at the nursery where his two and a half year old son Ryan, was safely tucked in his crib. He gently pushed the door open to peek inside, careful not to wake him. The room was gently lit from the glow of a small table lamp, surrounded by stuffed animals and books. The room was so quiet, he could hear his son breathing. He looked around the room and envisioned the trophies and awards his son would someday earn, as an all-star athlete in school. He thought about the joy of teaching his son the business that his father had taught him, that they too, would one day run together. Ron smiled at his sweet son, gently pulled the door back to the slightly ajar position and headed to his bedroom.

Ron's wife Karen was sleeping so soundly, he didn't dare wake her. He went into the bathroom and got ready for bed. He was exhausted. It had been a very long day, and he couldn't wait to crawl into bed. He looked at the clock – it was 2:45 am. He gently sat down on the bed, leaned over to kiss Karen on the forehead, gently rolled to his side of the bed, and put his head on the pillow. He closed his eyes for what seemed like just a moment, when the piercing ring of the phone jolted him awake. Ron quickly reached for the phone before the next ring. He looked over at Karen, but she was still sound asleep. Ron took the phone into the bathroom, cleared his voice and said, "Hello."

"Is this Ron Hushinson?"

Ron was a bit startled. "Yes, who is this?"

The voice on the other end sounded calm yet business like. Ron was still trying to get his bearings, feeling as though he was still asleep.

"This is Cedars-Sinai Hospital in Los Angeles. Your father was brought in about an hour ago. He suffered a serious heart attack."

An immediate rush of adrenaline flooded through Ron. His mind was racing and the questions he wanted to ask, were all jumbled inside his head. His mouth froze, he couldn't speak. It felt like an eternity before he finally uttered, "I'll be right there. Please, tell my dad, that I will be right there."

Ron hung up the phone. He grabbed the same clothes off the bathroom countertop, that he had just crawled out of, tried to shake out the wrinkles and put them back on. He glanced for a moment in the mirror to see if he was really awake, or if he was just dreaming. He used his fingers to comb down an unruly spot of pillow ruffled hair on the upper back of his head. Through his light brown hair, the silver blessings of time glistened ever so slightly, with extra emphasis at his temples. He turned on the water and ran his hands quickly underneath. He shook his hands off a bit, before splashing his face. He grabbed the hand towel off the counter and blotted his face. As he was getting ready to walk out the bathroom door, he did a double-take in the mirror at his brown, bloodshot eyes. He just shook his head, turned off the light and went downstairs to his office. He scribbled a note to Karen.

"Honey, the hospital called. Dad had a heart attack and it sounds pretty serious. I will let you know as soon as I know more. I didn't want to wake you or Ryan. I love you."

Ron rushed to the hospital. His heart was in his throat. His father was his entire world. They had been more like best friends, his entire life. They were always together, whether working, golfing, family vacations, or just hanging out. He had always encouraged Ron to reach for the stars, and with his support, he knew he could never fail. His mind was still racing. He couldn't help but feel absolutely paralyzed at that moment, knowing there was nothing he could do now, but standby helplessly and wait.

There were nurses buzzing around his father, checking his vital signs. The constant beeping of monitors, pierced through Ron's core. His father laid motionless, with tubes and wires all over him.

"Can someone tell me what's going on? How bad is it? What happened?" All the questions zooming around Ron's head finally materialized, and flooded out all at once. One of the nurses grabbed his fathers chart, and in the midst of writing, answered Ron.

"Your father was found by the housekeeper, lying face down at his desk. She called 9ll, and they rushed him in, but we don't know how long he was unconscious before she found him. The doctor will be in shortly to give you more information."

Ron just stood there stunned. Unsure how to make sense of the news, he began to feel weak in the knees. He pulled up a chair next to his father, sat down and put his fathers hand in his. Ron put his head down on top of their cupped hands and said, "Dad, I'm here. Please don't go. I need you." Tears began to fill his eyes. Listening to the sound of the heart monitor, and how slowly the beeps were to each other, Ron finally realized the severity of the situation.

Ron lifted his head up, and looked towards the hallway. He could hear the nurses out in the hall, talking in a low murmur, but he couldn't make out the words. He sat silently, still holding his father's hand, praying for a miracle. Suddenly, his father's arm twitched. Ron stood up, leaned over his father and said, "Dad? Dad? Can you hear me? I'm right here with you. You're going to be alright." He yelled to the nurses, "He's moving... someone... come in here!"

A nurse quickly came in, bent down close to his dad and said,

"Robert? Robert, can you open your eyes?" They both looked at him intensely for any signs of eye movement. The nurse checked his pulse and made sure all the wires were still hooked up properly. She smiled at Ron and said, "Some patients have involuntary muscle spasms from time to time, while others do start to move on their own, as they are regaining consciousness. It's hard to say which one it is right now. Hopefully he will open his eyes soon. Keep talking to him, he can hear you." She grabbed the chart, made a few notes, then she turned to walk out of the room. Just as she reached the door, she turned to Ron and said, "I am going to call the doctor and let him know that there was some movement. I will be at the nurses' station if you need anything."

Ron felt a bit of relief, as though this was a sign that his dad was going to be okay. He wanted to stay positive and believe that the movement meant he was going to wake up soon. "You gave me my own heart attack, Dad. We've got a lot of things yet to do, so you have to promise me, you'll get better."

About an hour later, the doctor came into the room. "Mr. Hushinson, I'm doctor Bradley. There is just no easy way to say this, so I'm going to be blunt here. Your father's heart attack was quite severe, and we're not sure yet if there has been any brain damage, due to the loss of oxygen. When the housekeeper found him, he was not breathing. Her quick response to administer CPR stabilized him until the paramedics arrived, however the crucial factor here is the amount of time before she found him and resuscitated him. We are still waiting on some of the tests to come back, then we'll know more. I would like to ask you, does your father have any advance directives? I know this is a subject that many people don't like to discuss, but it would be helpful to know, in order to proceed with his care and follow his wishes. Since his condition doesn't seem to be improving as of yet, and he didn't show any signs of movement during the reflex exams – well – I just think we need to be prepared either way. Once we get the other tests back, I will update you. I'm sorry I don't have better news."

The doctor turned and walked out of the room. Ron just sat there, staring at his dad. He seemed so frail. So vulnerable. Something Ron had never seen in his sturdy, healthy as a horse father. Robert was a very handsome man, solidly built, standing proudly at a height of six feet two inches. He had jet black hair in his younger days, which was now a full head of silver hair. His strong, chiseled facial features had softened over time, due to lacing effects of age and compassion. A much warmer look than the rugged, often stern looking younger version. They were very similar in stature as well as looks, and Ron had often felt honored to resemble him. Ron shook his head and closed his eyes. Hoping it was all some kind of bad dream, and he'd wake up at home. The smell of freshly brewed coffee and pancakes in the air, with Karen and Ryan in the kitchen laughing and smiling. Ron blinked a few times. *Nope*, he thought. *Not a bad dream. It's real. This can't be happening. This isn't how it's supposed to be.*

It was 8:30 am, and still no new updates about the tests from the doctor. Ron walked out of the room to call Karen. "Hey babe, did you sleep well?" he asked.

"Yes, but I was really startled when I woke up and you weren't here. Where are you? Is something wrong?"

"I'm sorry sweetie, I didn't want to wake you when I left, so I wrote you a note and put it on my desk. Didn't you see it? I'm at the hospital. Dad had a heart attack."

Karen was completely taken off guard. She gasped, "What? No, I haven't been in your office this morning. Ryan slept in, so I thought I would get a jump on the laundry. What happened? How is he? Is he going to be…" All of Karen's questions started flying at mach speed.

"The doctor says it's very serious. They ran some tests, but they haven't come back in to update me yet. His arm twitched, so I thought that was a good sign. They don't know how long he was unconscious or not breathing, so there might be some brain damage. I'm completely lost babe. I can't lose him..." Ron's voice cracked.

Karen tried to be reassuring but by the tone of Ron's voice, she knew this would be completely devastating to him. It would be the second loss for Ron, since his mother had passed away suddenly from a car accident a few years earlier. Ron and Robert had always been close, but when she passed away, it really brought them even closer. Karen knew that she needed to be reassuring, even though something deep within her felt the end was near. "Hun, he's in good hands. I'm sure the doctors are doing everything they can for him. Have faith. He's a strong man, just like you. He can pull through."

"Thanks sweetie, I know... it's just such a shock. I think I am going to head over to the office and look through his files and see if I can find anything – you know – in case we need to make any decisions. The doctor had asked me if I knew of any advance directives he might have. We never talked about this kind of stuff, so the office is the only place I can think of, where he would keep important documents like that. I'll call you in a few hours." He paused for a moment. "Hey uh, Karen? I love you!"

"I love you too, Ron. It's going to be alright. We're going to be alright. Just breathe."

Ron told the nurses that he was leaving, to go see if he could locate any of the documents they might need. He gave them his cellphone number, in case there were any updates. He headed over to the office in Sherman Oaks. The streets were congested with the usual heavy traffic. It's a town known for it's quaint little shops, trendy hot spots and large office buildings all slammed together. It's a property investors dream town.

He was driving down Ventura Boulevard in a daze, almost on

auto pilot, when he realized he was about to miss his turn. He whipped his car around the corner and his eyes locked on their sign, hanging out front of their majestic, four story brick building. The double sided sign was shaped like a shield and framed with black wrought-iron. It hung from an artistically sculptured black metal pole, with black chain on each side of the shield attaching it to the pole. The shield was his father's idea, as a *Protector for Truth.*

"Hush and Son Private Investigations."

His eyes filled up with tears. This business was his father's life. They built it into an extremely successful and well sought after company, with an impeccable reputation for their strong ethics, and desire to help people uncover the truth. This would be the company that he would hand down to Ryan one day. It was his legacy.

Ron pulled into the underground parking structure, and sat in his car. His head was running full speed with memories, and worries. He grabbed the car door handle, opened the door and stepped out of the car. He walked slowly to the elevator and went up to their suite. It was Sunday, so the offices were all closed. The only sounds in the building were coming from cleaning crews, bustling around the halls vacuuming, and the faint sound of music coming from a radio down one of the hallways.

Ron unlocked their office door, took a deep breath as he opened the door and walked in. The office walls were all covered in wood paneling. They had been beautifully decorated by Ron's mother Grace, who had a knack for decorating with very elegant touches. While a bit outdated to the current day's trends, neither Robert nor Ron, wanted to change a thing. It had a small sofa to the front right of the the room, with a small glass topped cherry-wood coffee table in front of it, and two matching side tables. There were two pub style brown leather chairs sitting opposite the small sofa. There was a tall ficus tree in the back left corner and an elegant corner shaped waterfall fountain in the right rear corner. They had it custom built to bring in the sounds of nature. Something that Robert really cherished. It helped remind him when he was in the office, of all the wonderful mountain hikes and family vacations in the great outdoors, that their family had taken when Ron was young. Ron's office was on the left rear side, and Robert's was on the right, nearest to the fountain.

He went into his fathers office and sat at his desk. He ran his hands over the top of the glossy, cherry-wood desk. He picked up one of the awards they had gotten from the City Counsel, for outstanding achievement in the community, for their volunteer works. He glanced over at the corner of the desk, at a picture of himself and his dad. It was one they had taken, when they put the new sign up on the building. They were standing in front of the building, his father's arm over his shoulder, looking up at the sign and giving a thumbs up to the camera. Ron was looking at his dad in the picture, pointing at him instead of the sign, with the biggest open mouthed smile he'd ever taken. He had to smile again, looking at the picture because he remembered exactly how he felt the moment that picture was taken. He chuckled out loud. It was a great day and had always been a fond memory for him.

Ron started opening the desk drawers one by one. Flipping through folders and files. Nothing. He stood up and walked over to a tall, five drawer cherry-wood file-cabinet that was on the wall alongside of the desk. Opening those drawers one by one, still not finding what he was looking for. Ron was growing more and more frustrated. By now the stress, worry and anger was starting to take over. He went back over to the desk, standing between the desk and the chair, leaned his hands on the desk and paused for a moment. His emotions finally took over, and he fiercely pounded his fists on the desk. He started feverishly pushing things off the desk and on to the floor. At that moment, he stepped back a bit and his legs hit the chair. He had so much extra adrenaline energy running through his body he needed to lash out. He turned around facing the chair and with all with his might, he shoved the chair with his foot, sending it flying full force into the wall behind the desk. As soon as the chair hit the wall, a hidden door in the wall popped open.

Ron stood back – visibly stunned. The door had been closed by a small magnet lock, and when it was shut, it appeared to be just a solid wall. Since the entire room was covered with light wood paneling, it blended in so well that Ron had never even noticed it. He pulled the door completely open and inside was a tall black file cabinet. He reached for one of the drawers and pulled on it. It was locked. He went back over to the desk to search for a key. He searched through all the drawers, but couldn't find it. He looked around the office, wondering where his dad would have hidden it. His eyes finally fixated on one specific picture, hanging on the wall. It had been there for as long as Ron could remember. *"Three things cannot be long hidden; The Sun, The Moon, and The Truth."* Ron took the picture down, bent the staples back that were holding the cardboard backing on, and removed it. On the other side of the backing was a piece of masking tape, holding a key. Ron went over to the the file cabinet and opened it. There were all kinds of files he'd never seen before in there. Dating back almost fifty years. They were all in off-white jackets, except for one. It was a very large folder, three times the size of all the others, and it was in red jacket. Ron grabbed it and opened it. Inside there was a handwritten note from his dad.

Son, if you are reading this, I can only assume that something has happened to me. I wanted to tell you this in person, but I just never found the right time. I am not proud of the man I once was, and I need for you to understand and forgive me. I tried to build a life for us, one that you would be proud of. You are my world. I have cherished you, from the moment your mother and I found out that we were expecting, and you were the driving force for me to become a better man. I don't know how to start, where it all began or why I did the things I did, but just know that this one file that you are holding in your hands, was the turning point in my life. It's what made me decide to change, and to become a better man and father for you. I wanted to build a business that was highly respected, one that we could share together, and that would be helping others. Let me just start – but please know that this is extremely hard for me to write, because I know it will come as such a shock to you. I hope it will help you understand why I turned my life, our lives around and devoted it to helping people find the truth, no matter what that was.

There was a time that I helped suppress people's indiscretions. It was very lucrative work, for very little effort. When I started out, I was young, single, and stupid. I saw an easy way to make money, and I lacked the ability to have empathy and compassion for others. I was driven by my ego and the rush of adrenaline I felt from this new-found attention. I fell into that line of work, pretty much by accident.

One friend asked me for a favor, then they referred me to someone else, and it just took off. People came to me to help them "erase" certain things, that if they had become public, might have caused great embarrassment for them. At the time, I didn't really stop to think if I was hurting anyone or not. People came to me, asked for help, so I did whatever I needed to, in order to get the job done. I didn't let it sink in. I felt almost detached, as if I was just an actor myself. Nothing in my life – up to that point, had taught me to really feel. To put myself in the situation, and look deeply at every angle, and learn that while we live our lives for ourselves, our actions do affect the lives of others profoundly.

As you read through this file, and the extensive added notes to help you understand better, please know that this part of my life was my deepest regret, as well as my biggest inspiration. It was only through that darkness, that I found the light. My light. My compassion and I learned what unconditional love truly is. I ask you to keep an open mind... and remember the man you knew. The loving, caring, father, grandfather – the man who would have given his life for you. But in order for you to remember those parts of me, I have to share the other side with you. And just as I learned that you have to know the whole story, the good and the bad, and embrace them both as part of this miraculous thing we call life – I hope you will see how we all have the choice, and those choices ultimately keep us locked up, or beautifully unlock the truth of who we truly are. This, my son, was the beginning of the legacy I leave to you.

Ron took the file, walked out of his father's office and over to the sofa across the room. He sat down, put his feet across the length of the sofa and started reading through the file. His eyes were getting heavy, the exhaustion had finally caught up with him. The adrenaline rush was now gone. As he relaxed while reading the file, he drifted off into a deep sleep, his mind playing the file as though it were a movie, while his own imagination filled in all the missing pieces.

CHAPTER TWO

It was a mild fall evening in 1966, and there was a slight Santa Ana breeze blowing. The Santa Ana's are warm dry winds that
descend from the high desert, down the San Gabriel and San
Bernardino Mountains and into the Los Angeles basin. The popular
Hollywood actors, better known as the "A listers," were gathering
together at a large Beverly Hills mansion that belonged to one of
the most powerful actors of the 50s and 60s. They were celebrat-
ing the final wrap of a movie that they were hoping would be an
"award winning film." The actors, producers, directors and some
of their close friends were getting together for the traditional
Hollywood wrap-up celebration. These parties were just one of the
many perks the children experienced, where they could hang out
and bond with other celebrity offspring, without being hovered
over.

A few of them were child actors themselves, but growing out
of the "child phase," and were about to embark on their own lives
in the industry, just like their parents. Most of them had already
graduated from high school, but there were some of the more
mature upper teens that were allowed to partake in the rituals,
whenever they were given the opportunity. The younger
generation however, chose to party away from the scornful eyes
of the adults. It was more fun to feel that they were in a world of
their own, without listening to the standard boasting of the adults,
and watching endless back-pats they gave each other about how
"this is one of the greatest movies they have made yet." Talks that
the kids were all too familiar with and quite bored of.

Christine was the beautiful, blonde hair, blue eyed daughter of
Edward, a "back-stager," who had worked for the studios for twen-
ty-four years. She knew many of the kids at the party, from when
they would hang out at the studio. Christine was invited to the

party by Jason, the son of one of the most controversial actors in Hollywood. Jason looked very much like his father. He was tall, and had the same intriguing blue-green eyes as his famous father. Jason's brunette hair came from his mother. He was muscular, and well built, but his insecurities kept him low key. She had known Jason for a few months, but this was the first time that they would see each other away from the sets. For Christine, who was just sixteen, this was a dream come true. She had told her parents that she was going over to her friend Jane's house, to work on a project for school. Christine borrowed her mothers car and drove over to Jane's house, which was only two blocks away from hers.

Christine was all smiles as she filled Jane in on her plans for the evening. She did however 'forget' to mention that her main reason for attending this party, was to see Jason. Jane was feeling a bit nervous to lie for Christine, since she knew that Christine's father was very protective of her. Jane was far more reserved in all aspects than Christine. She had shoulder length, blonde hair that was usually pulled back on the sides with clips, and she wore black framed, horned rimmed glasses. "What should I say if your parents call and ask for you? I mean, I don't understand what the big deal is. Your dad knows most of these people anyway. It's not like you're new to the whole scene," said Jane.

"Hey, don't worry about it, it's no big deal. I know they won't call, plus I told them that I wouldn't be home very late. My dad hasn't been real keen on these parties for a while, at least, not the ones where all the kids hang out by themselves. He's always saying that they're up to no good hanging out together. I heard him ask Charlotte once, why the kids didn't like hanging out in the house, and she told him that the folks are a real bummer to hang out with. My old man just doesn't get it, and I don't want to get any heat from him, by telling him that I wanted to go tonight. I just think the parties are a blast! Anyway, I'll leave my mom's car here, in front of your house, so if they drive by they will believe I'm here. They'll never know that I went to the party. All you have to do is drop me off at the party and I'll find a ride back to your house to pick up my mom's car."

Christine pulled a light blue dress out of her bag. The long sleeves were fitted from the shoulder down to the elbows, then flared out towards the wrist. It had a round plunging neckline, high fitted waist with a bow sewn on right underneath her chest, and short, flirty, flared bottom. Christine walked towards Jane's bathroom and said, "I'm going to get ready now, and then we can go."

When Christine walked out of the bathroom, Jane said, "Wow Christine, you look groovy. Are you trying to impress someone there or what?"

Christine just smiled as she pulled up her calf high white boots and said, "Lets boogie. I'm not sure how long it's going to take to get over there and I don't want to be late."

The sun was setting as the two girls drove over to the party. Christine and Jane were in awe just looking at all the exquisite homes in the neighborhood. They all seemed to have large, lush green yards. Some homes had tall wrought iron fences around them, and some had tall, thick bushes that acted as fences, that the girls could barely see over. The lights in front of some of the homes twinkled off the glass of the windows. There was a mix of Colonial style homes, beautifully crafted brick homes, and some that had a mix of both modern and traditional in their architecture.

"Check these houses out Christine," Jane said.

"I know, could you imagine living like this? I mean, how cool," Christine answered.

"Living in Encino, I thought that our houses were pretty bitchen, but seeing this is out of sight," Jane said.

As they were looking at the house numbers, Christine started getting more excited. Jane read the house numbers off of the
curb. Christine shouted out, "That's it." She pointed to the next
house. "That's it. That's the house. Pull over there Jane, just past
the driveway, and I'll walk up." She leaned over and gave Jane
a hug. "Thanks for the ride. I'll call you tomorrow and tell you all
about it." Jane started to say, "have a good time," but Christine
didn't hear her as she was closing the door.

The sense of excitement flooded over her as she walked up the
long driveway. For a few moments, she just stood there staring at
all the lights outside of the colonial, two-story house, and listening
to the laughter of the people inside. It looked as if it was a movie set itself. She walked up to the back of the cars waiting to be
parked by a valet. He pointed to the courtyard and said, "That's
where the hip people are," as he smiled and got into the car. She
walked through the gate on the side yard, towards the music and
laughter in the backyard.

She could feel her heart beating faster and faster as she got
closer to the group. She tried not to show how nervous she was,
but she felt that everyone could see that her knees were knocking
together. She pulled herself together a bit, and shook her hands
down by her side. She quickly wiped the perspiration from her
palms onto her dress. She realized that no one was really even
looking at her. She started feeling a bit more relaxed. She looked
around to see who was there and get an idea of how she could slip
into one of the groups and act as if she'd been there for a while.

She saw some kids by the poolside, dancing to the Beach Boy's
'Good Vibrations.' There was a smaller group of kids inside the
pool house playing pinball. Some were standing by a table full of
snacks, and some were sitting by the TV. As a couple ran by her,
towards the outside fire pit, she noticed a familiar face off in the
distance. There Jason sat, on a low planter wall – alone, waiting for

her. His dark brown hair shimmered in the moonlight. He was wearing blue jeans with brown boots. He had on a light weight, white,
button up shirt – a little over halfway buttoned. His shirt wasn't
tucked in, so it gently blew slightly in the wind. He was looking
down at the ground and he hadn't noticed her standing there yet.
She knew that it was too late to join one of the groups near her,
and act like she had been there for a while. She turned her head
slightly away from Jason's direction, but kept watching him out of
the corner of her eye, waiting for him to glance her way. As soon
as he looked up and saw her, she casually and slowly ran her
fingers through her long, silky blonde hair. Her heart was beating
so fast she thought she was going to faint.

She didn't want to appear too eager to see him and desper-
ately tried not to look his way. She decided it would look better for
her, not to just be standing there, so she started walking towards
the pool house. 'Wild Thing' by the Troggs, started playing on the
radio. She just kept walking towards the pool house. Just as she
was about to the door, a strong hand grabbed the back of her arm
and stopped her in her tracks. With her back still towards him, she
closed her eyes and took a deep breath. Savoring this moment,
she slowly exhaled, opened her eyes and turned to face Jason.

He gently put his hand on her waist, his touch – so intoxicating
to Christine. He stared deep into her baby-blue eyes. With a gentle
squeeze, he pulled her towards him and kissed her on the cheek,
ever so gently. "Christine, I was hoping you would come tonight. I
couldn't stop thinking about you."

Christine smiled and said, "I never thought that I would be
standing here with you, in your old man's backyard."

"I know, it's cool isn't it? I mean, we haven't spent a lot of time
together other than just messin around at the studio, but you
know, after we started kissing and stuff, I feel like maybe it could

turn into more. That's why I really wanted you to come tonight."

Christine replied, "Ditto, I feel the same Jason, but your old man..."

Jason interrupted her, "Don't worry about my old man. I have a right to my own life," Jason said.

"I know you do, but that look he gave us when he saw us coming out of the dressing room... I don't think he approves of his son – hanging out with the prop-masters daughter," Christine said.

"Don't worry about that. He always looks annoyed. I honestly don't even think he gave it a second thought. He's always so busy, he never even has any time for me or my brother Mark. Even though Mark's career seems to be taking off, I think he's just so focused on himself, he doesn't even know. Or maybe he does, and he's still upset that Mark and I wanted to get into the business. My old man never really wanted us to. I don't know if he's afraid we'll embarrass him, or if he's afraid of a little family competition, but – awe heck Christine, I don't want to talk about that junk. Let's blow this joint. I want to take you somewhere... somewhere that we can be alone. Somewhere that will be our place to escape to, and no one knows where we are. It will be just like the two of us are the only two people on the earth."

"Are you sure Jason? All your friends are here. Won't they miss you if you leave? I mean, I don't want to cause any problems for you," Christine said.

"Nobody is gonna miss me. Besides, most of these people are Mark's friends. They hang out over here all of the time. Really, it's no big deal if I flee the scene." Jason took her hand and led her away from the group of kids. "Come on – don't be silly, this is gonna be awesome," he said. As they started walking away, Christine heard her name being called from the other side of the yard. It was her oldest sister Charlotte. She was standing on the veranda, just outside of the house with her husband Peter. She had a few friends within the "elite" group, so she knew everyone too. Christine was shocked. She had no idea that her sister was going to be there. She had to think of an excuse quick, so she didn't embarrass herself in front of Jason, nor alert her sister into calling their dad. She told Jason to wait there, and she walked over to them.

"Hey, I didn't know you guys were gonna be here," Christine said nervously.

"I should say the same to you Christine," Charlotte said.

"Well, uh, I saw some kids at the studio the other day when I was with dad, and they told me that I should come hang out. I didn't have anything else to do tonight and I thought it would be a blast," Christine said.

"Oh, so dad knows you're here then," Charlotte said condescendingly.

"No, I didn't tell him I was coming. I remember hearing him argue with you one night about why you shouldn't come to these things, so I just didn't think it was worth getting him all upset over," said Christine.

Charlotte looked over to where Christine had been standing. She squinted her eyes as she stared at Jason. "Is that Jason Davis you were talking to," Charlotte asked.

Christine tried not to panic. "Oh, yeah, I was just talking to him a little bit. He said that he could introduce me to some of his friends, you know, just in case I ever wanted to pursue a career in acting or... well, you know."

Charlotte was used to Christine's wild behavior and she was uneasy with that story. There must be another reason Christine would want to come hang out with people so much older than she was. Charlotte had no idea that Christine even knew Jason. She had never mentioned him before, and she told Charlotte everything, she thought.

Christine tried to contain her overly anxious behavior so

Charlotte wouldn't suspect anything about she and Jason's 'real' relationship. "Hey, I gotta get back over there. Some of the kids were saying that there weren't enough drinks in the pool house so Jason and I were just gonna run out and get more sodas from Thrifty's. We'll be back in a little while, maybe we can hang out or something," Christine said.

Christine felt it better to tell Charlotte as little as possible because she didn't want to hear the lecture that she knew Charlotte would give her. Charlotte was quite a bit older than Christine, almost thirteen years older, and she acted a bit motherly towards her at times. Charlotte had short blonde hair, and blue eyes. Her style in every way, was very conservative.

Christine felt as though Charlotte herself had forgotten what it was like to be young and excited about life.

Peter, also uptight and conservative in appearance was no less in his demeanor. He gave Charlotte a look of disapproval, as he listened to Christine. Charlotte said, "I think there is a bit more going on than you're telling me Christine, and you know that dad wouldn't approve of you being here. Not to mention, he wouldn't be happy with me, knowing that I let you go off with Jason."

"Don't flip your wig Charlotte," Christine said. "I won't do anything to get you in trouble. I promise that I won't get home too late, and dad doesn't even need to know I was here."

Then Christine leaned in towards Charlotte's ear and whispered, "Why are you such a worry-wart, you aren't my mother you know."

Charlotte whispered back, "I know I'm not, but she wouldn't approve either. You know how she feels about her baby. You have always been a worry to her, and I always get blamed when you screw up."

With that said, Christine smiled a spoiled-brat kind of smile. "You two need to chill," Christine said and she ran back towards

Jason.

Charlotte and Peter just looked at each other in amazement. Peter said, "You know, she fits in perfectly with some of these kids. Brat to the core. Promise me our kids will never act like that." They both chuckled and went back inside the house to the party.

Christine and Jason walked slowly through the courtyard, occasionally pausing to stare into each others eyes. The trees overhead were draping over each other like a canopy, and they had little lights woven through them. As the wind would gently move the branches, it made it look like the lights were twinkling. The passion and longing that they both felt for each other was amplified by the ambiance of the night. The exhilaration of Christine's excitement was shadowed by a bit of apprehension. As they reached the end of the courtyard, they went through a large wrought-iron gate that lead to the front porch.

The front porch was decorated for Thanksgiving which was a few days away. There were sculptured trees in ceramic pots, covered in lights on each side of the large front door. There were a few small bales of hay on each side of the porch, with pumpkins sitting on top to add to the festive feeling. There was a large fall wreath hanging on the front door that had a horn of plenty resting on the bottom center, and a huge rust colored bow to finish it off.

As they waited for Jason's car to be brought around, Jason said, "You gotta check out the ride my old man bought me. When my mom, Mark and I, moved here to LA, he gave me and Mark one. He said that they were belated graduation presents. My mom said that they were 'guilt gifts,' since for the past twelve years, we had pretty much only seen him on holidays, or when he made the time for us. Pretty messed up, but whatever...They are primo rides."

Christine couldn't see what kind of car it was, because as it was being pulled up, the headlights were right in her eyes. They stepped off the porch and away from the headlight glare. Then she saw it. A 1965 convertible blue and white Chevy Corvette. Just as she was about to comment on how cool it was, they heard a loud roar of laughter coming from inside the house. "Someone must have told a far-out joke," Jason said. They heard all of the adults laughing and talking. Christine just looked at Jason and they both started laughing. Jason said, "At least you don't have to live with this every day. It gets old, you know. My old man has so many people around, kissing his ass, it's almost sickening. I know that he's a great actor, but sometimes just hearing these people complimenting him over and over just gets on my nerves."

Christine just smiled and nodded as if she knew what he meant. As the car stopped and the valet got out, Jason put his arm around Christine, walked her over to the door and opened it for her. He helped her into the car, then closed the door. Christine was shocked. She had never been treated with such proper manners before. Of course, she'd never dated a nineteen year old before, and for a moment, she herself felt like one of the elite. She thought, *Chivalry is alive*, as she smiled to herself.

As they drove away with the top down, Jason said, "Tonight, I'm going to show you the real stars."

They drove down towards the beach. The wind was whipping her hair around, so she grabbed it and held it in a ponytail with one hand. Her other hand was resting on the console between the seats.

Jason could sense that she was feeling a bit nervous so he turned on the radio and then rested his hand on top of hers. The new hit by the Beach Boys, 'Barbara Ann' came on the radio and they both started singing. They laughed and sang as the streetlights overhead slowly started to disappear.

The longer they drove, the more Christine started thinking. The thoughts raced through her head, faster than Jason was driving. She knew that she was young, and that his family was quite powerful. It all seemed like a fairytail though. She thought back to the first time she set eyes on Jason. It was at the studio. She loved to go hang out after school. Her father was the head of his department, and he was always busy making sure that everything was perfect on the set. Christine used to dress up in some of the costumes when no one was around, and dance around pretending she was an actress.

One day when Christine was walking out of the sound stage, Jason was walking in. They locked eyes with each other, but both of them just kept walking. The next day, Charlotte had to go to the studio to pick up some costumes that she wanted to borrow. She was painting a portrait for an art class, and needed the models to wear fancy clothes. Christine begged Charlotte to let her tag along. Christine looked all over the studio, praying that she'd see Jason. She had just about given up. She walked over to a small field nearby and sat under a tree behind one of the sets. She was looking down at the ground, picking small blades of grass and pulling them apart, when she saw feet stop right in front of hers. She slowly looked up. The sun was right behind his head so she could barely see his face. She moved her head slightly to block the sun with his body. There he was, just standing there.

He said, "Hi, I'm Jason. I saw you the other day, but when I came out of the set you were gone. I have been hoping I would run into you again."

Christine stood up so she could see him better. Trying not to be too mesmerized by his beautiful blue-green eyes, "I'm Christine," she said. "I have been coming here all summer, but since school started, I haven't been able to come as often. My old man works here."

Jason, not wanting to brag about his famous father, tried to down play his reasons for being at the studio. "Yeah, my old man works here sometimes too, and I just came with him to check some stuff out."

They talked for a little while and then they parted ways. They saw each other about once a week for a few months. They would run through the lots at the studio and they would hide in the empty sets. They kissed a few times but that was about all Christine thought it would ever be, especially after she saw him leave one day with his father. She was kind of taken aback when she realized who he was. She didn't mention it to Jason though. She thought that if she acted like it was a big deal, he would think that was the only reason that she was hanging out with him.

Christine also knew that if her father knew, he would forbid her to see him. She didn't want to cause a problem for her father at work, so she never mentioned her relationship with Jason to anyone. Even though she wanted to tell her friends at school, she knew that they wouldn't understand either. She had to hide a lot of things from her friends. They didn't all have the same kind of background. They wouldn't understand, and Christine didn't want them to use her either. They might want to hang out with her at the studios, just because it seemed so cool. Jane was really the only one that Christine felt semi-comfortable with.

Jane knew that Christine's father worked at the studios, but Jane was not really interested in that. She was a real bookworm. Jane's father was a lawyer, so she had more money than the other girls at school too. Christine met Jane one day while Jane was walking her dog by Christine's house. Christine was washing her mother's car. Jane said, "That doesn't look like fun."

Christine laughed and said, "Yeah it's not, but it's the only way my old lady will let me borrow it when I learn how to drive." Christine introduced herself to Jane and learned that she had just moved in. Christine and Jane were instant friends. Christine thought about how Jane covered up for her tonight and she knew that without Jane's friendship, this night would not be happening.

As the car pulled up at the beach, she felt her heart inside her throat. This was definitely changing everything, being alone with Jason. No one around to walk in on them. No hiding behind sets. Just the two of them.

They walked in the sand barefooted, holding hands for a while. Jason was carrying a blanket in his other hand. He stopped and turned towards Christine. He dropped the blanket at their feet. He looked deep into her eyes, as he brought her hand up to his lips. He kissed her hand so gently. As he slowly lowered her hand, he leaned in to kiss her neck. She could feel his breath in her ear. He slowly kissed her neck and moved towards her ear. He sighed a gentle sigh. He put his arm around her back, holding her gently, but firmly. She could feel goose bumps all over her body. He whispered in her ear, "I have been wanting to be with you since the first day our eyes met."

Christine was a bit unsure just exactly what was about to happen, but she had a tingling in her gut. Somewhat excited, nervous and scared, yet at the same time calm and at ease.

Jason laid out the blanket on the sand. He knelt down on the blanket and smoothed out some of the sand bumps. He took both of Christine's hands in his and gently pulled her down onto the blanket next to him. They embraced, and sank into the blanket on the sand.

CHAPTER THREE

For the next few weeks, Jason and Christine met at the studio, snuck out to meet each other at the movies, and met at diners. Christine was feeling like she was on top of the world. She truly loved Jason. This was a feeling that she had never known before. Between the feelings of excitement and butterflies in her stomach, she hadn't really had much of an appetite. Sometimes she felt as though she could just cry she was so happy. She wondered though, how long the two of them could sneak around.

Jason was also feeling the pressures. His father was starting to get suspicious. Mark and his girlfriend tried to set Jason up on a couple of blind dates, but he would always make up an excuse to get out of it.

Jason was in his first year of college, as a film major. This part of the business was his real passion, but with his new interest in Christine, it was very difficult to concentrate. Christine was a junior in high school, and she too was having a hard time concentrating. She would just stare at the clock waiting for the bell to ring so she could rush to be with Jason. Christine's friends were getting excited for the upcoming winter formal at school, but Christine couldn't share their enthusiasm. She wanted to take Jason, but didn't dare ask him to go. She counted the days until winter break, when she and Jason could hang out together.

Finally, it was Friday, the last day of school before the break. The bell rang and the kids were running through the halls of the school cheering. Christine cleared out her locker and started to head towards the parking lot. A few of her friends were talking about the dance when Christine walked past them. "Hey Christine, are you going to the dance tomorrow?" one of the girls asked.

"No, I can't. My family has plans to go out of town," Christine said.

"Oh bummer. It's gonna be a blast," another one of the girls yelled as she ran ahead of the group towards the cars.

"Yeah, I know. Well I hope you guys have fun," Christine said as she turned and walked away from them.

The girls just shrugged their shoulders and continued their conversation.

When Christine got home she noticed Charlotte's car in the driveway. She hadn't seen Charlotte since the party.

Charlotte had stopped by the house to pick up some boxes of clothes and other things that she had been storing at their parents house. Now that they were in their new home, she had plenty of space to keep their things. There was a large box that had her wedding dress in it, and a few smaller boxes of old baby clothes from her children.

Christine went into the house and headed towards her room. She could hear Charlotte in the kitchen on the phone.

As Christine walked past Charlotte's old room she saw the box with the wedding dress in it. She started to walk into the room, paused, then she bent backwards and stuck her head out of the door to listen to hear if Charlotte was still talking on the phone. *Yep, coast is clear.* She walked over to the bed and grabbed the box. She picked the dress up carefully, lifted it out of the box and held it up to herself. She walked over to the the full-length mirror in the corner of the room and just stood there for a minute. She turned one way, and then she turned the other, never taking her eyes off of the mirror.

Meanwhile, Charlotte had finished her phone call and headed toward her old room. She heard Christine talking, so she slowly crept up to the door.

Charlotte was standing at the corner of the doorway but Christine didn't notice that she was watching her.

Christine gazed into the mirror dreaming of the day she and Jason would get married. She whispered the words, "I do."

Charlotte burst out laughing.

Christine threw the dress onto the bed. "Man Charlotte!! Don't sneak up on me like that. It's not cool," Christine snapped.

"Who are you, I-doing to?" Charlotte asked as she picked up the dress, folding it back up, to put in the box.

Christine looked at Charlotte and asked, "What's it to you?"

"Well I was just wondering if it had anything to do with a certain someone that you were at a party with a few weeks ago," Charlotte said jokingly.

"Hey Charlotte, nothing was going on, and nothing is going on. I swear you and Peter have such big imaginations," Christine said sharply.

"Wow, you're a bit snappy aren't you Christine? I mean for goodness sake's I was just messin with you," Charlotte said.

"Yeah, whatever, you go ahead and make your jokes..."

Just then Christine caught a glimpse of the clock on the nightstand, through a reflection in the mirror. She suddenly realized that she was late to meet Jason at the park. "Gotta jam," she said as she bolted to the kitchen to grab her mother's car keys.

Charlotte yelled, "Christine, does mom know..." just as the door slammed shut. She walked over to the bedroom window and looked out. She saw Christine getting into the car and heading down the street.

As Christine drove down the street a ways, she saw her parents driving up the street. Her father Edward, slowed the car down and started to roll down the window. Christine turned up the radio as she was bobbing her head to 'Bang Bang' by Cher, looked towards her parents, smiled, and kept on driving.

Edward and Priscilla looked at each other and shook their heads. Edward was a tall thin man, with light brown hair. Priscilla was extremely petite. She was only five feet, two inches tall. She had short, dark brown hair. Even though their heights were so dramatically different, they complimented each other with their clean cut Cleaver-esque presentation.

They drove up the street and Priscilla said, "You know Edward, she really needs her own car."

"Yes dear," Edward sighed.

"She'll be seventeen in a few months anyway, but it's not just that, the most important part is, I can't have her simply taking my car whenever she wants. Lately, it seems like it's been all of the time."

"I know dear. I have been thinking about a car for her, but she hasn't been doing all that well in school lately. I feel like she should prove to us that she deserves it," Edward said.

They pulled up in the driveway of their classic traditional home, that screamed standard suburbia. Complete all the way down to the yellow paint and white trim, with the outlined yard with it's white-picket fence. They grabbed a few bags of groceries out of the back seat. As they were walking into the house Edward said, "Well dear, we made it through two girls, only one more to go." He chuckled and Priscilla rolled her eyes.

Just then Charlotte came around the corner and said, "Excuse me? If you are insinuating that Diane and I were as uppity as Christine, you are sadly mistaken," Charlotte quipped.

"Oh right, you don't remember some of the crazy things you put us through? However, you are right. Christine has been a bit more secretive than the two of you were. It seems like she's been keeping something from us. She disappears all the time, she didn't want to go to the winter formal at school, and I hardly see Jane over here anymore," Priscilla said.

The three of them walked into the kitchen and started putting away the groceries. Charlotte said, "I haven't really had much time to talk to her lately, but you're right, she is kind of secretive."

Edward chimed in, "Well when I take her to the studio with me, she seems fine. She talks to me all the way there. She seems just fine to..." Edward stopped in mid-sentence remembering something that Christine had done at the studio. "Come to think of it, she disappears. I don't see her until it's just about time to go. I asked her once why she likes coming to work with me. I know that it gets boring being there such long hours, especially on the weekends, when she should be hanging out with her friends. She says that she hangs out with the make-up artists. She thinks it's 'cool.' Priscilla, maybe you should talk to her. If something's going on, we should try to help her. You know, a lot of kids are smoking marijuana and drinking at parties these days, maybe she's gotten in with a bad crowd."

"Dad, let me talk to her. I know that I'm not around much, but when I am here, it seems like we don't seem to talk like we used to. I tried to talk to her today. She was playing around with my wedding dress. I made a joke and she got all offended. I thought is was just me. Then all of the sudden, poof, she was gone. Do you guys think that she's still upset that I got married, moved out and had kids? I mean for the most part, she's kind of been like an only child. You know, come to think of it, Christine was seven when I moved out. That's the same age as my little Scott is now. Wow, now I feel old," Charlotte said shaking her head.

"I don't know if that's it or not Charlotte." She paused for a moment and counted the years Christine was the only child living there. "Perhaps there is a little truth to that. Diane left not too long after you did. I guess that it is a little different having sisters that don't live in the same house as you growing up... I never really thought about it much," Priscilla said.

"I think that she is just acting out. You know, kind of rebelling, and trying to get attention," said Edward.

"I do think that's part of it. Plus, Diane only comes home from school to visit once in a while. We aren't here to hang out with or just chat with like siblings usually do," Charlotte said.

"Well, maybe she does miss you Charlotte. You and Christine were a lot closer than she was with Diane. They just don't have as much in common. They never really have been that close," Priscilla said.

"Okay, well, before you accuse her of drinking and doing drugs, let me talk to her. She won't feel like we are all ganging up on her that way, and maybe we can get to the bottom of all this before Diane comes home for Christmas," Charlotte said.

Christine drove to the park to meet Jason. She was elated. Jason was sitting on a swing when she pulled up. She got out of the car and ran over to him as she screamed, "Winter break is finally here." She flung her arms around his neck as she said, "Hey, how's it goin'? Sorry I'm late, I had to ditch my sister. She stopped by the house to talk to my mom."

Jason stood up from the swing and gave Christine a big hug, actually picking her up off of the ground. "I've been missing you a lot lately," Jason said, " I have something for you. I heard this song the other day, and it reminded me of you. 'When a Man Loves a Woman,' by Percy Sledge. Have you heard it?"

"No I haven't, but I can hardly wait to hear it," Christine said eagerly.

Jason handed her a small bag with a 45 record in it. He took Christine by the hand and walked over to a tree. He sat down and leaned his back against it. Christine sat in front of him, between his legs, with her back towards his chest. She scooted back and pressed up against his chest.

He held Christine with his legs pressed up against hers, and rubbed her shoulders. They snuggled tightly and watched the sun set as they talked. Jason told Christine that he had to go away for a few days with his dad. "I'm going to Santa Barbara this weekend to watch Mark perform in a play. I wish I could take you with me. I'm really not looking forward to the drive with my dad. I can hear him already, riding my ass because he thinks I'm not focusing on film school as much as I should be. I mean, he is right, I do have a hard time concentrating sometimes, but I don't think I am doing that bad. Mark wants me to start acting with him, but that's not really me. I'd rather produce and direct. I think that I'm more of a behind the scene kind of guy."

"I know that you are talented Jason, and I know that you'll be awesome in whatever you do. Just make sure that you're happy. Don't let your dad or your brother push you into something you don't want to do," Christine said.

"You know, after my dad re-married, he has really been hard on me and Mark. I don't know if it's because he has a new family now and we don't get to spend as much time with him, or if it's just me. I mean, Mark and I kinda feel that it's because he is so famous, he expects us to be just like him. We are 'his sons' and we live under a microscope. But for me, it's like the pressure of living up to his expectations is really bummin me out. I am so afraid of disappointing him, or making him look bad, that I have a hard time putting my heart into anything. I'm not as outgoing as Mark is either. He seems to make everything he touches turn to gold. I know Mark struggles with trying to please him too, but at least he knows how to jump bad, like my dad, to stand up for himself. You know, he has already performed in a couple of plays, and word has it, he's got what it takes to make it in Hollywood. Mark has always told me that he didn't want to ride my dad's coat-tails, but I think it's more than that. My dad is known as a real bad-ass. He knows what he wants and he gets it. Not that many people can stand up to him, including me. I don't think that Mark wants that kind of reputation though," Jason said.

"Well can you blame him? I've heard stories about your dad too. I've heard people talking after he walks off the set. The things they say aren't that nice, and I don't think that anyone would want to follow in those footsteps. Don't get me wrong, I know that he has done some fantastic work, and he is very talented, but he really does scare me. Did I ever tell you that he saw me coming out of his trailer?" Christine asked.

"No. Are you serious?" asked Jason.

She started to tell the story and she reminisced back to the day. She could feel her palms getting sweaty all over again. "It had been one of the days that you and I were hiding in the sound stage. Some of the crew hands had come in, so we ran out the side door. You had suggested that we stop by your dad's dressing trailer, that was parked way out in a field, to grab a soda. You said that since they were filming out in the field, he wouldn't be there. When I stepped inside the trailer, I got kinda freaked out. I looked around at all the pictures of your dad in some of his films, and of him with some other actors at a party. They were smoking cigars and they had drinks in their hands. I read the caption on one of the photos. It said, 'The night we won.' That must have been after one of the award ceremonies. I could smell his cologne mixed with cigar smells, and again, the uneasy feeling became unbearable. You were looking through a cabinet for some snacks, and you weren't really paying much attention to me. I opened the door and ran outside. Just as I had closed the door and had walked down the trailer steps, your dad pulled up in one of the studio carts, driven by a stage hand. He gave me a hard look as he turned to the driver and said, *'Let me get the old script. I think that scene was written better before, cool your heels, I'll be right back.'*

I had already started walking away from the trailer by then. I kept fearing that he had seen me come out of the door. I was waiting to hear your dads reaction to you, for being in the trailer. I thought for sure he would be yelling at you if he would have seen me. I walked up on that small hill far enough from the trailer, but close enough to catch your attention when you came out. Your dad came out of the trailer five seconds later, with a big pile of papers in one hand, and a lit cigar in the other. Then he said, *'I can't believe I forgot this damn thing. I've gotta do everything around here. Now back to the set, time is money,'* as they drove away. When you stepped out of the trailer a minute or so later, you had two bottles of coke and some pretzels. I waved to you and you walked up the hill. Remember, you asked me how come I left. I told you that I just needed some fresh air?"

Jason, thinking hard said, "Oh yeah, I remember. I heard the door shut, but when I looked up, I didn't see you."

"Yeah, and I didn't know if you had seen your dad come in or not, and it seemed obvious that your dad just grabbed whatever he was coming back to get, and that he didn't see you either. I decided not to mention anything to you about the close call. I didn't want it to freak you out and spoil our day."

As she finished telling Jason the story, she turned her head around to see his reaction, but she couldn't tell by his face if he was mad at her or not. "Are you mad at me for not saying anything?" she asked.

"No, of course not. Don't be silly. I just wish you would have told me. I mean, it was a close call and all, but I think that I would have tried to be more careful, if I would have known." He turned her all the way around and kissed her forehead."Don't worry, everything is copacetic baby," Jason said.

"Well, I did know what a close call it was, so I made sure that I was careful for the both of us," she said.

It was getting late, and Christine remembered that she had just run out of the house earlier without really telling anyone where she was going. She had forgotten all about Charlotte and the wedding dress scene. She knew that she'd have to come up with some kind of story to tell her mother. She and Jason made plans to get together when he got back the following week.

"I'll miss you babe," Jason said as he held her tight.

"I'll miss you too Jason. Think about me when you're gone," Christine said with a laugh.

He walked her over to the car and opened the door for her. They kissed and hugged and she got in the car and drove away.

When she pulled into the driveway and got out of the car, she noticed Charlotte sitting in her car, getting ready to pull out of the driveway. She rolled down her window. "Where have you been miss-moody," Charlotte asked.

"Oh I realized that I promised to meet some friends at the park. I had completely forgotten about it when we were talking, and then it just hit me. Where are you off to?" asked Christine.

"I am going to pick the kids up from the sitter and then we are meeting Peter's parents for dinner. I'll be back tomorrow, I wanted to talk to you. Are you going to be around in the morning?" Charlotte asked.

"Yeah, I don't think I'm going anywhere. Dad said he's leaving kind of early for the studio. I've been having a hard time waking up in the morning lately. He said that he didn't need me to help him this weekend anyway," Christine said. Knowing that the real reason she didn't want to go to the studio was because Jason wouldn't be around.

"Well, I want to talk to you, so make some time for me, okay? Hey, by the way, you didn't steal that record did you? You've been holding it behind your back, but I can still see it," Charlotte said with a chuckle. Then she drove away.

Christine went into the house. To her surprise, her mother and father were sitting in the living room with a strange look on their faces. "Do you have something you want to tell us young lady," Edward asked.

Christine's heart leaped right up into her throat. *Oh my gosh,* she thought, *do they know? Had Charlotte seen her at the park and said something? Did they find one of the notes Jason had written her, that she had hidden underneath her dresser drawer?* "Uh, what do you mean," Christine asked as her voice cracked.

Priscilla said, "We just got a phone call from…"

Oh my gosh, here it comes, I'm dead meat. Thoughts just raced through Christine's mind. *I wonder who blabbed. I wonder if my dad is going to lose his job. I should just turn and run. Ah come on, they don't know, no one could know.*

Just then Priscilla said, "Your art teacher. She called to tell us that you painted a mural for your final, and she loved it. She said that you have a lot of promise as an artist. Well Edward, I guess it runs in the family huh?"

"Your mother and I are very proud of you. If you want, you could start taking classes to help develop your skills. I mean, I could teach you, but I haven't been painting as much lately since work has been so busy. Charlotte would help you too, if you asked her," Edward said.

Christine, still trying to compose herself after thinking the worst, uttered only a few words. "I don't know if painting is for me. I mean, you and grandpa are great artists, Dad. Charlotte and Diane are too, but they have a different style of painting than I do. I mean, they are really talented. I don't think I could be like them, and I don't want to be compared to them either," Christine said.

"You don't have to be compared to them. Everyone is different, and your sisters have been to some of the top art schools. You haven't even graduated from high school yet. Give it some time," Edward said as he stood up and kissed Christine on the forehead. "Your mother and I have been thinking that maybe it's time you had your own car too. You have done pretty well in school this year, although the past few weeks leave much to be desired, but you've shown a lot of maturity lately. If you promise to focus, and pull your grades back up, I think we can work something out. Plus, your mother is sick of you just taking her car whenever you feel like it," he said as he walked out of the room.

"Are you serious Mom, I can have a car?" Christine asked as she could hardly contain herself.

"Yes dear, your father is going to start looking at some cars tomorrow after work. He said that he is only working for a few hours in the morning, so the afternoon is open to start this project. Who knows how long it will take to find something for you," Priscilla said.

"Well, Charlotte said she was going to come over tomorrow. She said that she wanted to talk to me. I'll call her and tell her to come another day," Christine said as she headed for the phone.

"No, you go ahead and go with her. Have a good time with your sister. You don't see her much anymore, and I think it would be nice for the two of you to get out and do something together for a change. If your dad wants to buy a car for you, he will, whether you are there or not," Priscilla said as she rubbed Christine's back.

The next day, Charlotte picked Christine up. She pulled up to the house and honked. Christine ran out of the house with a piece of toast in one hand, still brushing her hair with the other hand. She jumped in the car and threw her brush into the back seat.

"Wow, you weren't kidding, you really must be having a hard

time getting up in the morning. It's like 10:30 am Christine. Maybe you shouldn't stay up so late at night," she said as she messed up Christine's hair. "You know we haven't really gone anywhere together in a long time. I'm going to enjoy hanging out with you today." They started driving, the windows were rolled down and it was an unusually warm December day. "The weather is so nice I thought we could just drive somewhere and enjoy the sun," Charlotte said.

The car was too quiet so Christine leaned forward to turn on the radio. Just as she pushed the button for the KHJ radio station, the song that Jason had just given to Christine came on.

"Oh I love this song," said Charlotte, as she started to sing.

It looked like they were driving towards the beach. *Is this cruel irony?* Christine wondered. *First the song, and now the beach. The exact same beach that Jason and I had been at, one month before?* She thought... *No way. This is not happening. Why would she pick this beach, of all places to go.* They pulled up and parked.

As they got out of the car, they walked down the beach a little way and talked. Charlotte, trying to be cautious with her words said, "You know Christine, we have not had a lot of time together lately to just talk. I feel bad. I wanted to know how you are doing and what's going on with you. I noticed that you weren't going to the winter formal tonight with all of your friends. In fact, I haven't really seen you hanging out with anyone in particular in a long time. I know that there have been a lot of changes lately, and you probably feel like an only child since Diane is away at school, and I am busy with the kids and trying to get my art work off the ground."

Christine, started to feel sick to her stomach, wondering why her sister would pick this beach to come to. On top of missing Jason terribly, and not wanting to be at their beach without him, she tried to compose herself and strike up a conversation. She looked out at the waves, tipped her face towards the sun for a moment and then sat down. "You know Charlotte, it's not about any of that. I know you guys have your own lives, and I'm happy for you. It's nice that you and Peter are getting your lives in order, and mom and dad are happy for you too. Your paintings are starting to take off, and it seems like the world is just waiting for you. I, on the other hand, am not sure what I want. Dad said that my art teacher called him, she said that I have promise. I'm just not sure that is what I want to do with my life. Everything seems like it's spinning out of control, and it's really not. Have you ever felt like you weren't in control of your own body? Like a puppet or something? That's kind of how I've been feeling. I go to school, I look at my friends, and they are all having a bitchen time. I go to class, and I just drift off in my mind. I can't concentrate on anything. I'm not going to the dance because I don't feel like I have anything in common with any of my friends anymore. It seems like they have all changed or something," Christine said as she kept looking out at the ocean.

"Maybe it's you that's changed," Charlotte said. "Maybe you're growing up and they seem naive and childish to you. I think that it has made you grow up a lot faster having Diane and I as older sisters. You know it's not all that uncommon to grow apart from your friends. Just don't grow apart from your family. Remember that we all love you, and we want you to be happy," Charlotte said as she leaned over to hug Christine.

CHAPTER FOUR

The nice warm days were gone. Winter break was beginning to feel more winter-like. Edward was outside hanging Christmas lights on the front of the house. Priscilla was in the house with Christine setting up Christmas decorations in the living room. Christine took the family pictures off the oak mantle and replaced them with a manger scene. She put the snowmen that her mother made several years earlier, on one side of the brick hearth. Then she put a poinsettia up on the other side of the hearth. "Not too close to the opening of the fireplace," Priscilla said, "I don't want to worry about anything catching on fire."

Christine pushed everything farther out to the sides. "There is that better?" she asked.

"Yes Christine, that's good." She quickly glanced around the room, smiled and nodded. The rust colored sofa was directly opposite the fireplace and on both ends of the sofa were oval shaped oak side tables. They both mirrored each other with the same brass candle holders sitting on top. They held three red candles each with the center one being the tallest, tapering down in size. The matching oak coffee table was decorated with cotton sheets that looked like snow. In the center of the 'snow' there was a good sized mirror that held several figurines wearing ice skates. The Christmas tree was off to the corner of the room. It was almost as tall as the ceiling. "I think that there are enough decorations sitting around don't you? Let's decorate the tree now," said Priscilla.

As Christine took the glass ornaments out of the boxes, she remembered how old some of them were. "Wow Mom, we still have these?" Christine asked as she held a few up to her mother. There were several different designs on these ornaments. One had a Christmas town painted on it that they had gotten from Christine's grandparents. There were several others that were given to the family by relatives throughout the years. Most of them, who had passed on now. Each girl had their own personalized ornament that Priscilla hand made for them. She had written their names on the ornament with glue, and rolled them in glitter as a reminder of their first Christmas'.

"I hate to throw any of them away. I remember every single one of them. There are even a few from mine and your fathers first Christmas together. I don't put those up though. I have them wrapped special and I just look at them when I pull the rest out," Priscilla said.

Christine helped her mother put the tensel on the tree and then the lights. Next came the ornaments. "Mom, why don't you just hand them to me, and I'll put them on the tree," Christine said.

Christine and her mother were almost done decorating the tree. "Just one more thing," Priscilla said. She handed Christine the tree-top ornament. Christine stood up on a chair to put the star on top of the tree. Suddenly she felt amazingly dizzy. She tried to regain her balance, as she pushed up against the tree. The tree started to tip backwards until Christine regained her balance. A few of the glass ornaments fell off and clanked on the floor.

Priscilla looked up and said, "Christine, are you okay? Be careful, you don't want to fall and break your arm for Christmas do you?" she joked. She smiled at Christine and put the fallen glass ornaments back on the tree. "Maybe the antibiotics the doctor gave you the other day aren't working."

Christine finished putting the tree-topper on, stepped down off the chair and helped her mom put the unused decorations back in boxes. "I'm going to my room to lay down," Christine said as she was walking away. She had been feeling so tired the last few days, she thought that maybe she was coming down with something different than the strep throat the doctor suspected. As she drifted off to sleep, she dreamed of a warm day at the beach with Jason. Just the two of them dancing in the break of the waves, with the wind blowing gently and the sea gulls flying overhead. She felt the warm sun on her skin, and Jason's arms holding her tight. She could feel the cool ocean spray on her face and could taste the salty water in her mouth. She and Jason, holding hands, spinning around in the wet sand as the water just brushed their feet. Laughing and laughing. She threw her head back and she had her arms around Jason's neck, his hands were wrapped around her waist. Around and around they spun. Spinning, spinning, laughing, and spinning.

Just then she quickly sat up, ran to the bathroom and threw up. Her head was spinning and she was extremely nauseous. When she could finally control her stomach, she crawled back into bed. About an hour later, her mother came into her room. "What's the matter Christine? Do you feel like you're coming down with the flu now?"

"I don't know Mom, I just don't feel good. I've been really tired lately and I can't seem to shake it," Christine uttered.

Priscilla felt Christine's forehead and said,"Well, if you aren't feeling better tomorrow, we'll go back and see the doctor. His office should have called already with the results of the tests he ran two weeks ago. You seem to be getting worse."

The next morning, Christine woke up to the same nauseous feeling she had the day before. She went into the kitchen to get some crackers. Her mother came into the kitchen and felt Christine's forehead. "You still feel a little warm honey. Are you feeling any better?" Priscilla asked.

"Not really Mom, this is a real bummer. I was supposed to meet a friend today that I haven't seen in a while," Christine said with a depressed tone.

"Well, you're not going anywhere now, young lady. I am going to call the doctor and see if we can get you an appointment this morning. Just go lay down and I'll get you up when we need to go," Priscilla said.

"But Mom, I need to take a shower. I think my hair smells like barf." She let out a sigh. "Maybe that will make me feel better," Christine said as she walked down the hall to the bathroom.

Christine went to get ready and Priscilla made an appointment. After Christine got out of the shower, she went into her room and called Jason to tell him that she wasn't feeling very good. "I know I shouldn't be calling your pad, in case your dad is there, but I have to go to the doctor this morning. I think I have the flu, and I don't think I can meet you this afternoon."

Jason was very disappointed. "Don't worry about calling here, my old man never comes by my place. I hope you're okay. I've been looking forward to seeing you for the past three days. I really wanted to show you my new place. This separation has been really hard for me."

Christine replied, "Ditto Jason. This has been really hard on me too. I think that maybe it is just the flu or something. I promise that I'll call you as soon as I get home. Maybe the doctor can give me a shot, and we can still hook up later tonight." With that said, Jason told her to feel better and they hung up.

Just then, Christine heard her mom calling. "Doctor Murphy can see you in forty-five minutes so hurry up. I need to finish my Christmas shopping before tonight. Charlotte is picking Diane up at the airport and they are coming straight here."

"What's with the urgency to finish all your shopping. You still have a few days until Christmas," Christine shouted from her bedroom.

"I just have a few things to get for our Christmas party, and I want it to be special. Diane hasn't been home for a while, and I feel like I need to make our Christmas party really something special this year," Priscilla yelled. "Now hurry and finish getting ready."

As Christine and her mother drove to the doctor's office, they didn't speak. Christine just held her head in her hands. Priscilla looked over at her occasionally and rubbed her head. They parked the car on the main street and went into the building. They walked into the doctor's office. Christine went to sit down while Priscilla signed her in. As the nurse called Christine into the room, her mother said, "I'll be back in a little bit, I'm just gonna run a quick errand." The nurse led Christine to the exam room. She took Christine's blood pressure and temperature. She asked her a few questions and left the room. As she sat there looking around, she started thinking about what she and Jason could do for Christmas. Trying to think of a story to get her out of the house, so they would be able to sneak away to spend some time together. With Diane home, and Mark home, both families would probably be spending a lot of 'quality time' together. Christine's idea of quality time would be hanging out with Jason, alone!

Just then the doctor walked into the room. "Hello Christine," he said. "I hear that you're still not feeling well. I had thought you might have strep throat – which the antibiotics I prescribed for you last time would have taken care of, but the tests I ran came back, and it's not strep. Tell me what you're feeling and what's going on with you."

Christine explained, "Well, I have been really tired for the past few weeks, and I feel sick to my stomach. I've been getting dizzy too sometimes, when I stand up too fast."

"Alright Christine, there's a good explanation for this. I already know what's wrong with you. I'm going to try to jog your memory a bit, and see if you can figure this out too. Let me ask you, do you remember when your last period was?"

UGH! How embarrassing. I don't want to answer that, she

thought. *You're a guy. That's personal!* She just sat there staring at him, not quite grasping at his hints.

"Christine, when was your last period?" he asked again.

She let out a big sigh. Realizing this question was going to continue being asked until she answered, no matter how much she resisted. "Um, I think it was about the end of October, beginning of November," she said quietly.

"Right. So, depending on when, it's nearly two months later, and that wasn't concerning you?" he asked.

"I've been kind of preoccupied. Lots of things going on right now for me, I guess I just lost track. Why?" she asked nervously.

"Christine," he said, "I've been your doctor since you were a little girl. I stitched up your knee when you fell off your bike. I took out your tonsils when you had all those throat infections. I have seen your sisters both grow up into wonderful young women. It's important for you to know I am on your side. Knowing your family for such a long time, I really wish you would allow me to invite your mother in to talk this over."

"Doctor, tell me first – what the hell is wrong with me, and then let me decide if I need you to fill my mother in," she snapped.

He looked down at his file and gathered the strength to say it. "I feel bad that I have to tell you this – at least at this point in your young life – Christine, this is not going to be easy to hear..." he paused. "You're pregnant."

"I'm what?" she said as her eyes filled up with tears.

"You're pregnant... I'd guess about a month or so, and by my calculations that would make you due sometime in August. Now, I know that you are almost seventeen and feel like you're all grown up, and you can handle this, but really..." He paused for a moment, realizing Christine wasn't in the mood for a lecture. "I know deep down inside you are probably in shock right now and need time to process this. I would really like to help you break the news to your mother – that is, if you would like me to. I know that there must be a lot running through your head right now, and perhaps I can help ease the tension a bit, and buffer, if you will, this news. I know how your mother can be. But before you answer my question, can you think of any questions for me?"

She just sat there. No facial expression what-so-ever. The stream of tears that flooded her eyes started running down her cheeks. She felt that at that moment, her life had just ended. What was she going to tell her mother and father. *Oh my gosh,* she thought, *they are going to be so mad. They'll disown me. How could this happen to me,* she thought. Just then she gasped. *Jason! He's never going to talk to me again.* Her eyes filled up with even more tears instantaneously.

At that moment, the only thing that she could think about or really care about, was Jason and his reaction. How am I going to tell him? Then another rush came over her. Her heart fell into her feet. *His father. His father would kill him.*

Just then the nurse walked in, "Christine, your mother is back, I'm going to call her in. Is that okay?" she asked. Christine just sat there. Her head hung low. The nurse looked at the doctor questioningly. The doctor nodded his head, signaling the nurse that she should go get Priscilla.

Christine heard her mother's voice ask the nurse if everything was alright. As she entered the room, the silence was almost deafening. The doctor told Priscilla to have a seat. "Christine, tell your mother," he said. Christine tried to hold back the tears, but she just couldn't.

"Mom," she said with a timid, cracking voice.

"What Christine, what is it?" Priscilla asked.

"Mom…" Christine paused, took a deep breath, and stuttered out, "I'm, I'm, I'm pregnant." Christine sobbed uncontrollably.

Priscilla sat there for a moment stunned. "There must be some kind of mistake doctor, this can't be happening. Do the test again," she demanded.

"Priscilla, the tests I ran a few weeks ago are accurate. I am sorry, but this is happening."

"Christine! How could this happen? When? With who? I just don't understand. Do you have any idea how this is going to break your father's heart?"

The doctor stood up and he walked over to Priscilla, "Your daughter needs some support right now," he whispered. "You will have plenty of time to talk this over, but right now, I think she could use a motherly hug." Priscilla turned around to reach for her daughter, but Christine jumped off the table and ran out of the room.

The doctor said, "Priscilla I think that it would be a good idea to get some counseling. This is a very difficult situation, and I believe that you need to talk to a professional, trained in situations like these."

Priscilla agreed and got the information for the counselor from the nurse and walked out of the building. She had expected to see Christine standing by the car, but she was nowhere in sight. She started to worry. *Where could she have gone?* Priscilla went to a payphone outside of the doctor's office and called Charlotte. "Have you heard from Christine?" she asked.

"No, why, what's wrong," Charlotte asked.

"I'll call you later, I have to call your father, and I need to find Christine. Oh and Charlotte, do you think that you could just take Diane back to your house tonight? We can all get together tomorrow, I'll call you..." Priscilla said, as she quickly hung up the phone. She got into her car and drove straight home. As she was driving, Priscilla found it hard to keep the tears from pooling up in her eyes. She could hardly see the lines in the street through all of her tears. Her baby's life had forever changed. She'd never be the same again. She started thinking about all the things that Christine would miss out on. Then she thought about her own personal humiliation that she'd be subjected to among her own friends and groups too. The tears grew to small streams that ran down her cheeks.

When she pulled up in the driveway, there was a convertible yellow VW bug parked in the street in front of their house. She slowly walked through the front door.

"Hey honey, did you see the car I bought for Christine today? I got if from a guy at work. He bought it for his wife, but she said it wasn't big enough for her and the kids, so he had to get rid of it, cheap. It's only a year old, and it's in really good shape! She's going to love it isn't she?" Edward rambled on.

Priscilla tried to compose herself and break the news to him. "Honey, we need to talk." He was still looking out of the front window, just staring at the car and feeling proud of the great deal he just made, not really paying attention to Priscilla's concerned expression.

"Edward," she said again, a little more sternly. "We need to talk. Can you come over here and sit down?" He turned and caught her tear stained face and realized something was wrong. "I took Christine to the doctor this morning. I have some bad news – our baby – Christine..." she stalled and stammered, as she shook her head.

"What is it, dear? Out with it already," Edward blurted impatiently.

"She... she... she's pregnant."

"Where is she?" he asked.

"I don't know. She ran out of the doctor's office before I had gotten these counseling papers." She held up the packet to show him. "When I went outside, she was nowhere in sight. I didn't know what to do, so I just came home," Priscilla cried.

Christine had to get in touch with Jason. She called his apartment first, but he didn't answer. Then she called his father's house. The maid said he wasn't there and that she hadn't see him for a few days. Christine tried to call the studio, but he wasn't there either. She had been using a payphone that was outside a little strip mall, a few blocks away from the doctor's office when she looked up and saw the bus that would take her to the park by her house. Their park. The park that they would meet at in the middle of the night, where no one could find them. She thought if she just went there, she could get her thoughts together and figure out what to do next, before going home and facing her father.

She ran towards the bus, but just as she was going to get on it, she heard a car honk.

"Christine. Hey Christine!" Jason shouted.
She waved her arm at him to turn around. He made a 'U' turn in the middle of the street and swung his car around behind the bus and she hopped in. "Christine, what's wrong?" Jason asked. "You look so upset."

"What are you doing on this side of town? I've been calling all over trying to find you,"she snapped. "Just take me to the park. We need to talk. I want to be in a place I feel safe."

"I was headed over towards your house. I was gonna do a slick drive by, hoping you'd be standing outside," Jason said.

As they drove to the park, Jason was getting nervous. He kept looking over at Christine, who had her head turned away from him, looking out of the side window. She couldn't even look at him, for fear he would guess what she was going to tell him, and trying to wipe the tears away from her face, without him noticing.

After he parked the car, they walked to a spot where the trees were thick. The wind was blowing and it was cold. Christine had on a big sweater, but it wasn't very warm.

"Christine, take my jacket, you look cold. Look at you, you're shaking," Jason said as he put his jacket over her shoulders.

"I'm not cold, actually, I'm kind of numb. Jason, my whole life just came crashing down around me, and I don't know how to tell you this," Christine said nervously.

"Tell me what? Is it something you found out from the doctor? What did he say is wrong with you?" he asked.

"Jason," she took a deep breath and looked into his eyes. "You know that I love you, and I don't expect anything from you. Sometimes life just isn't fair and things happen that are out of our control, or that we don't expect to happen. The doctor ran some tests on me, and... well... I'm pregnant. The doctor told me that he thinks I'm due in August. My old lady was there, and she is so mad at me. She didn't even care about how I was feeling or what I was thinking, and went straight into a guilt trip, like I did this on purpose or something. Then she said that this was going to break my old man's heart. Like I don't know that? As if I'm so out of touch with the fact that it's always about them? Everything is and always has been about them, and their perfect little world. A world they'll now blame me for ruining. Oh man... I am so scared. When she started going off on me, I didn't know what to do, so I just ran out of the office. I left my old lady just sitting there. I don't want to face her, I don't want to face THEM! She's probably already called my old man, and he's probably on his way home," Christine said quickly.

Jason interrupted, "Okay, slow down. Is this for sure? I mean they did actual tests on you?" he asked.

"Yes, what am I going to do? What are YOU going to do?" Christine asked with tears rolling down her cheeks again.

"Don't you mean what are WE going to do? I am in this just as much as you are. Did you think that I was just going to bail on you or something? Yeah, it's kind of a bummer that it happened this way, but..."Jason paused. "I love you, and I think that we should get married."

"I love you too Jason, but I don't want you to marry me because you feel like you have to. I wanted you to marry me because you want to and because you love me. I can't marry you this way. What if you changed your mind later, or felt like you were trapped into it? Plus, what would your dad say? Tell him you knocked up a sixteen year-old and you want to marry her and see! He'd never stand for that and you know it," Christine said sharply.

That thought had not yet passed through Jason's head. "Oh shit... my old man..." Jason said with despair.

Christine and Jason decided that she should go home. When they got into his car, Jason told her that her mother was probably worried sick about her. They drove to the end of her street. "I'll call you later," he said. He stopped the car and leaned over and kissed her gently on the cheek. He said, "I don't want you to freak out. I'll always be here for you. I promise you that you won't go through this alone." She opened the door slowly and got out. She closed the door without even looking back at Jason. He looked up and saw her back turned towards him. Jason drove away. As she stood there for a few moments, she knew that the worst was yet to come.

She started walking up the street. When she got home, she walked right past the VW Bug and didn't even see it. She stood at the front door. She couldn't make her feet move. She was frozen. Just then the front door opened and her mother called to her. Christine walked slowly into the house. "Where were you?" her mother asked. "I was worried."

"I just needed some time to think," Christine replied.

"I'm not really sure what to say to you Christine. This is such a shock. Your father is in the living room. Go in and sit down. We need to talk," her mother said.

Christine's father was a man of few words when it came to emotional issues. He found it hard to look at Christine. "You know this is going to alter our whole family Christine. Our reputation in this community has just been jeopardized by your selfishness." Edward stood up and walked over to the mantle. "I have worked hard my entire life to provide for this family. This is not acceptable behavior for one of my daughters. You have shamed us!" he said loudly.

"Dad, I'm sorry. I didn't do it on purpose. Don't you think that I know how this is going to affect you? There's a lot you don't know Dad, and I'm not really sure how to explain it," Christine said.

"Well you had better start trying young lady," Edward said sternly.

While Christine gathered up the courage to fill her parents in, Edward turned around, walked back over to the sofa and sat next to Priscilla. Edward and Priscilla sat there, listening to the story.

"For the past few months, I've been seeing this guy. I met him one day at the studio. I didn't know who he was at first, but we had such a great time together, I didn't really care when I did find out. His name is Jason Davis," Christine said.

"Keith Davis' son? Christine, don't tell me it's Keith's son," Edward said.

Christine interrupted, "Dad, just let me finish. Yes, it is Keith's son, but Mr. Davis doesn't know anything about me. No one knows. Back in November, Jason invited me to a post wrap-up party that his father was having. You know, the ones where all the kids hang out, away from the parents. I didn't tell you that I was going, because I knew that you wouldn't let me go. I just thought that Jason and I were having such a great time hanging out, that it would be fun to see him away from the studio. Charlotte and Peter were there, to support her old friend from school. I had no idea they were going to be there."

Edward stopped her, "Charlotte knew about this?"

"Not really Dad. I did see her at the party, but Jason and I left. I didn't talk to Charlotte about that night, and she never questioned me about it either. Anyway, Jason and I have been seeing each other after school and on the weekends, every chance we get. It's not like a one nighter or anything," Christine said.

Edward went numb and Priscilla nearly fainted. The only thing that kept going through Edward's head was his career. *I'm going to lose my job*, he thought. As Christine finished her story, she just sat there waiting for her parents to say something, anything. This was definitely not the kind of Christmas present any of them had hoped for.

CHAPTER FIVE

Jason knew he needed to talk to his father. He procrastinated as long as he could, but he knew his time was running out. He feared that Christine's father would contact Keith directly first. He had to gather the strength to break the devastating news to the one person he admired the most and feared even more.

Tonight is the night he thought, as he slowly drove over to his father's Beverly Hills home. He knew that his father and stepmother would still getting ready for the big Christmas Eve party. He slowly drove up the driveway and pulled around back, to the garage area. He wanted to slip in the back door, but there were too many caterers around. He walked around to the front, and as he walked through the front door, he instantly felt sick to his stomach. He thought to himself, *here I am, trying to build a relationship with the father whom I hardly know, and now I am going to destroy it in one night.*

Jason looked around at the Christmas decorations. There was garland wrapped around the banisters, and the crystal chandelier was decorated with mistletoe. There was a twelve foot fully decorated Christmas tree in the living room, with mounds of gifts stuffed underneath. He just stood there and thought, *my family is going to disown me.* The house was elegantly decorated for their big Christmas celebration, which was a Davis tradition every year.

The entire family was going to be there, as well as a few close family friends. Jason tried to get there before anyone else did, so his father wouldn't cause a scene, but he didn't quite make it. Mark was already there, in the parlor with Keith. Jason walked from the living room towards the parlor. He peeked around the door and said, "Dad?"

Keith didn't hear him over the laughter, as he was saying, "Pour yourself another drink Mark and tell me more about the play."

Keith had light brown hair, and greenish blue eyes. He was no taller than five foot ten, even though he claimed he was six foot. He kept himself in fit physical condition, as many of his rolls required him to be shirtless in several scenes. Mark's looks and stature mirrored Keith's almost to a tee. They both had distinct cheekbones, and strong jawlines. The very 'look' that seemed to be what defined the 'heart-throb' male actor perfectly.

"Dad," Jason said again a little louder. "Can I see you in the library?"

Keith turned and looked at Jason with a curious expression, "Sure Jason," he said. "Mark, you can tell me about that later, we'll be right back."

Keith and Jason walked away. Keith had one of his hands on Jason's shoulder, the other hand was holding a glass of Jack Daniels. "What's the matter, son? You seem worried about something," he said as they went into the library.

Jason closed the doors behind them. Keith sat down behind the desk. They could hear some of the guests arriving. Keith's wife Erin was greeting them, and escorting them into the living room. Mark followed Erin and the guests into the living room and turned some Christmas music on that filled the house. Jason was finding it very hard to concentrate.

Keith stared at Jason and knew that something was wrong. "Come on son, out with it," he said sternly.

As he cleared his throat Jason said, "I have a problem Dad, and I need your help."

Keith chuckled and said, "You've never needed my help before, Jason. What did you do now?" he asked as he raised his glass to take another sip.

"Well, I've been seeing this girl... Uh... for a while... and uh... at first it was just like we were kind of messing around... and uh...,"

Just then Mark opened the doors to the library. "Is this really a 'private conversation' or did you just want to escape the crowd pouring in the door?" Mark asked.

Jason said, "Mark, can you just give us a minute?"

"Sure, I'll wait in the living room with the others. I was just bein' nosy. I didn't mean to interrupt," Mark said, as he closed the doors.

Keith proceeded to light a cigar. He leaned back in his chair and put his feet up on the desk as he said, "Come on son, out with it. I've got guests to attend to."

Jason fumbled with his words. "Uh, well, like I was saying Dad, I've been seeing this girl and well, um, she's in trouble Dad."

Not really paying much attention to Jason, Keith asked, "What kind of trouble?"

Jason took a deep breath realizing that he needed to just spit it out, and get it over with.

"Dad, this is hard for me to talk to you about, but... this girl... her name is Christine, well, I got her pregnant."

Keith nearly choked on his drink. "What the hell Jason...," he yelled. "You knocked up some little slut?" Keith stood up and put his cigar in the ash tray. "Do you know what this is going to do to my career? Such a scandal now will bring negative press. How could you be so careless Jason? I thought you knew better than that. Your mother and I have always told all of you, what you do is a direct reflection on us," Keith said, barely controlling his anger.

Jason knew that he had to just keep going. "Well, that's not the worst of it. Her father is someone that works at the studio. Not just some stage hand or anything, he's the head of his department, and he's been employed there for years. His name is Edward McMillan.

"You knocked up a nobody?" Keith muttered under his breath as he shook his head.

Jason didn't hear him and just kept talking, "The biggest part of the problem is that she's sixteen, I mean, she'll be seventeen in a few months."

With that statement, Keith flung his glass against the wall where some of the family portraits hung, hitting one with himself, Mark and Jason as little boys. The glass shattered into little pieces and the picture frame cracked as it smashed onto the floor. Erin and Mark heard the glass break and Keith's voice growing louder. They ran towards the room and when Mark slid the doors open, they heard, "This is a fine mess you've gotten us into, now how the hell am I going to get out of this," Keith barked.

Mark and Erin quickly entered the room and Mark closed the doors behind him. Erin had strawberry blonde hair that was just below her ears. She had dark brown eyes and was just slightly shorter than Keith. Erin walked over to Keith. She lifted her hand to touch his shoulder, and he jerked his whole body away from her, and continued to yell at Jason. "I can't have this kind of scandal in my life right now. I'm in the height of my career. This is not going to sit well with the industry, or my fans. You're barely out of diapers yourself boy! She's a minor, and this is crime. What if she claims you raped her? What if her father presses charges? This entire mess could land you in jail! She's got to get rid of it. That's all there is to it. You've got to tell her to get an abortion."

Jason replied in shock, "Dad, they're illegal. I can't ask her to do that! Besides, I love her. I'd never ask her to do that. She would never press charges against me..."

Keith quickly interrupted him, "So what they're illegal. They still do them. Knocking up a minor is also illegal – but you did that. You don't love her, you don't even know what love is. I won't hear anymore about this. I do not want my first grandchild being born of such scandalous circumstances. It must be destroyed!" Keith looked at Mark. "Mark, is Dan here? I need to talk to him immediately."

Mark trying not to look too shaken said, "I think so Dad, let me get him."

Mark brought Dan into the room, shut the door behind him, and sat down. Dan was about five foot four. He was trying in vein to hide the fact he was going bald, by combing over the remaining hair – that he kept fairly long – over to one side. His overly bloated ego and arrogance was the only thing about Dan that wasn't lacking.

Jason stood in the corner of the room, looking out of the window. Erin walked over to a chair next to Mark and sat down. Dan walked over to the desk and Keith sat back down in his chair, put his elbows on the desk and then put his head in his hands. "Dan, you're my best friend as well as my lawyer. Something has just been brought to my attention, that disturbs me greatly." Keith lifted his eyes to Dan. "I know that if anyone would know how to fix this situation, it would be you. I have too much at stake, and I need to make this problem disappear."

Dan tried to read Keith's face as Keith looked towards Jason.

Jason could feel his father's eyes burning through his back, so he slowly turned his head in his fathers direction.

Keith put his head back in his hands. "Damn-it Jason," he mumbled.

Dan looked over at Jason as well, and saw the humiliation and regret, written all over Jason's face. Keith asked, "Who do you know."

 Dan assessed the situation and he quickly realized that whatever the problem was, there was clearly an urgency to fix it. "I do know a guy. His name is Hushinson," Dan said. Keith took his hands away from his face and looked up at Dan. "He can fix anything. Whatever it is, it's no big deal Keith, really. He's gotten rid of... well, handled quite a bit of... Uh... indiscretions, that never leaked out to the public. I believe he calls it the 'Hollywood Hush.' He's discrete, guarded, and well, just plain ruthless. I'll make a call, day after tomorrow, and we'll take care of it, whatever it takes. I'll give Hush your number and you can discuss the situation directly with him." Dan leaned over the desk and patted Keith on the shoulder. "Is that all you needed? Cause I believe there is a party in the other room that we need to get to," Dan said with a lighthearted tone. He opened the door and walked out of the room, closing the doors behind himself.

Keith stood and looked at his wife, and sons. "None of this goes anywhere, you got me? If I'm gonna clean this up Jason, no one, I mean NO one, not even your mother can know. This night never happened."

Jason tried to explain a little more, "Dad, I understand that I let you down. I have disgraced you, and I am sorry, but I can't abandon her. It's not fair. I told her I would call her, I love her Dad, I asked her to..."

Keith cut him off. "Jason, I'll take care of it. But..." as he raised his hand and shook his finger at him. "You may not interfere in this. You could make more of a mess out of this with your good intentions. I trust Dan. I'd trust Dan with my life. He's honest with me and he has taken care of my career for twenty-five years. I won't have you destroy our family, your flesh and blood, not to mention my career, because of one mistake. This will be fixed, and we will go on. Don't you forget that!" And with that being said, Keith took Erin's hand, walked over to the doors and flung them open. "Oh yeah, and tomorrow is Christmas, I expect the day to be wonderful for David and Ellis. Your younger brothers don't deserve to have their Christmas ruined because of your stupidity. Be here at 3:00 pm. Mark, are you bringing that delightful girl you met at school? Keith didn't even wait for a reply from Mark. True to form, he put on the act of his life, as he walked out of the room, as if nothing was wrong.

Jason looked at Mark who was still sitting, stunned. "What the hell did you do," Mark asked.

"I got this girl in trouble. But it's not just any girl. I love her. I really love her. We've been seeing each other for a few months. I asked her to marry me and she turned me down. I have no idea how this is going to affect her family. Her father works at the studio, that's where I met her. She is really groovy. I really dig her. We have so much in common... I just can't believe that... it's gonna end like this," Jason said as he shook his head, visibly shattered.

Mark stood up and walked over to Jason. He put his arm around Jason's shoulder and started to guide him out of the room. "Someday, this will all be a faded memory, Jason. Just trust dad. This will blow over and we will be fine. David and Ellis will never know about this, mom will never know about this, and dad will eventually forgive you. Our 'family' will go on. Just don't disobey him," Mark said. Jason and Mark walked out of the room and into the party, trying to put on the same stunning performance that their father had.

It was Christmas afternoon. Mark and his new girlfriend Donna were in the living room with Mark's two younger half-brothers. They were playing a card game on the floor. Erin was buzzing around the kitchen making sure that the finishing touches were done properly for their dinner. Keith was upstairs looking over a script. He had a hard time focusing on reading it though. He was wondering how the meeting with Dan and his 'Hush' man would go. Keith had never felt that a problem was out of his control. That was, until now. He had to pull himself together and have faith in Dan. He was more unsettled now though, after Dan needed more information to give 'Hush' before they spoke. Having to explain the sorted details to Dan, cemented the dilemma even more in his nerves. He gazed at some pictures on the dresser of himself with the all his boys. He thought about how much he had missed out on Mark and Jason's lives after the divorce from their mother. Then he thought about the fact that his first grandchild would be brought into the world as an illegitimate child. The thought sickened him. The more he thought about it, the angrier he grew. His first grandchild... the scandal... Just then he stood up and he threw the script across the room hitting a large glass vase on a small wooden table. The vase crashed onto the floor, as the flowers and water went everywhere. He waited for someone to come rushing into the room to see what all the commotion was about, but no one came. Keith slowly walked out of the room and closed the door behind him. As he walked down the stairs, he told the maid that there had been an accident in his room. "Clumsy me, I broke a vase. Clean it up for me hun," he said. The maid just rolled her eyes and walked up the stairs.

Keith walked into the living room. "There are my favorite little men. Are you ready to open presents," Keith asked the little boys. David was eight. Two years older than Ellis. David had brown hair and sparkly blue eyes. He looked more like Keith than Ellis. Ellis looked almost exactly like Erin. He had the same strawberry blond hair and brown eyes. Mark and his girlfriend Donna were sitting on the sofa looking through a family photo album. Donna was an aspiring model. She had long, dark brown hair that was slightly curled at the ends. She had light brown eyes and was always 'made up' as if she were getting ready to walk down the runway of a fashion show.

Erin came into the room. "Jason isn't here yet? Shouldn't we wait for him?" she asked.

"I told the boy 3:00 pm. No respect! You know how I hate waiting for people. I'm gonna let David and Ellis start opening some of their gifts. Look how patiently they've been waiting," Keith said as he walked over to the tree and pulled out some of the smaller packages.

Just then Jason walked into the room. "Sorry I'm late. I went by my mother's house for breakfast, and we got to talking and I just lost track of the time." Keith looked hard at Jason to see if he had any guilt on his face. "She said that she's getting ready to go out of town for a movie shoot. It sounds really exciting for her. Mark, she said that you and Donna were going to go over there after you leave here."

"Yeah, I talked to her yesterday. I told her that I wanted to introduce Donna to her," Mark said.

"Enough of that," Keith barked. "Let's open presents."

They all opened a few gifts until they heard the chef ringing the bell from the dining room. "Oh good, dinner is ready," Erin said. Donna, Erin and the younger boys walked into the dining room first. David and Ellis sat down and waited for the adults. The dining room was impeccably decorated. In the center of the ceiling hung a three-tiered crystal chandelier.

The dining table had been custom built and could seat twenty people. It was covered with a rich, deep red table cloth and had a delicate white-lace runner in the center. From the China to the stemware, not one single touch was missing. Beautiful crystal candelabra's toward each end of the table, and an elegant bouquet of white roses mixed with dark red poinsettia's, baby's breath and fern.

"Oh this is stunning," Donna said as she looked at the lavish table setting.

"Thank you, we bought this set in Europe last year," Erin said as she took Donna's arm and walked her over her seat. Donna sat down as Mark and Keith were still walking into the room talking.

Keith and Mark stood at the doorway watching the women talk. "Well they seem to be hitting it off rather nicely," Keith said to Mark as he signaled towards Erin and Donna.

They continued talking as they walked to their seats. Keith was at the head of the table, and Mark sat to the right of him. "Yeah, she's a great girl. We really hit it off too. She's been getting a lot of work lately modeling, I think she might even be up for the cover of Vogue," Mark said.

Jason was the last one to walk into the room. He walked past the two of them, feeling a bit left out, and sat down at the table next to David.

Keith lowered his voice and leaned over toward Mark. "Well, do you think this relationship will turn into something more serious, son?" Keith asked.

"How many girls do I bring around for the holidays, Dad?" Mark asked in a whisper while flashing a quirky smile.

After dinner, Keith took Jason and Mark into the study and closed the door. Erin and Donna entertained the younger boys in the living room with all of their new toys. Keith walked over to the window and with his back to the boys said, "Look, I know that I lost my temper yesterday, but this is not something that I was prepared to deal with. I hope that the two of you will understand the lengths I will go to, in order to protect my family." He turned and looked at them. "Mark, I am so proud of you and your acting career. I know that you will go far. Jason, I know that you have only been in school for a few months, but I have faith in you, that you will dig in now, and put all your efforts into learning the business front and back. I want the three of us to work together. Nothing would make me happier," Keith said.

"I thought that you didn't want us following in your footsteps Dad," Mark said.

"Yes, there was a time that I thought it would be a bad idea to have my sons take the same path, but, I feel that the industry is changing and there is more to offer you boys, than there was when I got into the business. I know that I'm known as a real bastard, but I think you can use that to your advantage," Keith said with a half-smile.

"I'll do my best to make you proud of me Dad," Jason said.

"I know you will son," Keith said. He walked over to Jason and patted him on the back.

"Let's go check on the ladies, shall we?" Mark asked. He turned and opened the doors. Mark walked out of the room.

Jason started to walk towards the door when his father's back-pats turned into a stern squeeze on his shoulder. Keith spoke in a low stern tone, "Don't disappoint me again, Jason."

The next day Dan called Keith from his office. He said, "Your problem is solved. I talked to my guy, and he just needs a little more information, then you are off the hook and Hush will take over. He needs the name of the girl, her father's name, and... well... this is the biggie. What are you prepared to offer them for their silence. He said that he needs a 'back-up' plan, if he can't convince her father to abort the child. He seems to be in agreement with me that this little problem will cause just as much embarrassment for their family as well as yours. No one these days wants to air this kind of dirty laundry. I'm sure he wants to bury it too."

"Damn it, I don't care about their family Dan," Keith barked, "I don't want to give them a fucking thing. If his daughter would have kept her legs shut..."

"Look Keith, I know how you feel, but this isn't helping your situation now. Get past the anger and seriously ponder exactly what you are willing to do, if this guy won't get rid of the kid," Dan said. "You have to get real here. The way I see it, you only have two options. Playing hard ball will only work to a certain extent. Either they agree to get rid of the problem completely, or they give the kid away. Keeping it is not something you can overcome, and if they know this, they just might, out of spite. I'm not saying they will, I am just saying that if you don't make them an offer they can't refuse, the ball will be in their court."

Keith pulled himself together a bit. "Well, Erin and I were talking, and she had a feeling that we might have to step up with a little something to convince this guy of our point of view. This is a big sacrifice on our part mind you, but if it will help entice Mr. McMillan to leave town, we're willing to give them our cabin in Lake Arrowhead, along with a lump sum cash payment – with the agreement that both families will be free from any ties to that kid. We really just want that girl out of here during this mess. If she won't abort, pay them off and get them the hell out of here – just give them whatever it takes. I can't risk her being around, and Jason keeping his word that he won't contact her. But Dan – just make sure you put the emphasis on the termination," Keith said. He could feel himself losing control again, as he just kept growing angrier and angrier.

"Okay, just relax," Dan said, "Give me their information, and Hush can get started putting the heat on them. He feels the best time is now, while they're still in shock too. They'll be more vulnerable and easier to strong arm."

Keith had called a contact from the studio and had gotten Edward's information. He pulled a piece of paper out of the nightstand and read Dan the information he needed.

"I'll call you after the initial communication has taken place. We should have a better idea where they stand. It's probably going to be in a day or two considering that this is the day after Christmas and all. Just relax until then, and try to enjoy the holidays," Dan said, as he hung up the phone.

Dan turned around in his chair and across from him sat the mysterious dark-haired gentleman. He had a mustache. His dark brown eyes showed no genuine emotion. His aura was as cold as ice. He had a cigarette in his mouth and he was taking a drag. He blew out the smoke and looked at Dan. His name was Robert Hushinson, but a select few knew him as the "Hush man."

"Give me all of the information you have on these people," Hushinson said. "I'll do a background check on this guy. I'll check into his finances and see what else I can lean on. I'll find his weak spot and press on it until he caves. I'm going to get in his head. He won't be able to look anywhere without seeing my face. He'll see me in his sleep. He'll see me when I'm not even there. I'll make him so uncomfortable he'll gladly leave town on his own accord."

"I have no doubts in your abilities Hush, and I want to make sure you know there are no holds barred here. I was instructed to tell you to do whatever it takes," Dan said.

"Don't worry about it. I know that if someone needs my help, it's always urgent. I have never failed any of my clients or their 'problems.' Everyone gets my immediate attention. I'm proud to work with industry folks. It makes my job easier. Everyone is secretive. I can just get in, do my job and get out. I do have to admit, that this is the first time I've encountered 'this' particular situation though. Not that I have any doubts in my abilities, or that I can't get the job done. It's just that usually there aren't this many people involved, you know, less people to lean on. This will take a whole new level of – shall I say, 'talent,' and I'm looking forward a successful outcome," Hushinson said. He stood up, grabbed the paper with all the information on it and started to walk out of the room.

"Good man Hush. Mr. Davis has been a close friend of mine for years, and I want to make sure that this 'situation' is handled quickly, quietly, and professionally. This could actually open the doors of success for you as well, as I know Keith's allegiance to those who do right by him is very strong," Dan said.

Mr. Hushinson turned to Dan just as he was closing the door

and said, "I've never let anyone down, and I've never been one to gloat. I'll just let my reputation do my bidding for me."

CHAPTER SIX

Christmas at Christine's house was just as tense as it had been at Jason's. Her family was having their traditional family feast. Christine stayed in her room for most of the day, while Priscilla made the meal, set the table and swallowed her tears. After the big blow up, Christine had kept herself away from her parents prior to the party, but the occasional meeting in the kitchen would happen. There were few words exchanged between the three.

Priscilla went into Christine's room and said, " I know that you aren't really in the party mood, and we aren't really either, but no one knows what's going on, and I need you to get dressed and put on a happy face. We are going to go on as if nothing is wrong, and after Christmas, we will handle this situation."

Christine looked at her mom. "Situation," she said.

"Not now Christine, not now," her mother said as she walked out of the room to finish the last minute dinner details. Just then, Christine saw car lights pull up in the driveway. She heard the doorbell ring, and the sound of her parents' squeals of excitement. Priscilla opened the door with such excitement and said, "Diane, Oh Diane it's so good to see you. Just look at you. You look so great."

Diane resembled Priscilla almost to a tee, except for her height. She had taken more after Edward, standing at five-foot eight.

Everyone piled through the doorway and headed into the living room to sit down. The kids made a bee-line straight to the Christmas tree, plopped down and started taking inventory of the gifts.

Edward was standing by the fireplace, and as Diane walked closer to him he said, "School teaching you anything new kiddo, or am I just funding some new fad in Paris?" Edward wrapped his arms around Diane and hugged her.

As Diane and Edward hugged, Priscilla was walking into the room. Charlotte, Peter and the kids all complimented Priscilla in unison, about the wonderful smell of dinner.

"Wow Mom, this looks so beautiful and it smells incredible," Charlotte said.

"Hi Grandma," all of the kids shouted as they jumped up from their seats and ran towards her. Scott was the oldest grandchild. He was almost eight. He was the spitting image of Peter. Katie was just a year younger. She had dirty-blonde hair that was a little longer than shoulder-length. Timothy was almost five. He looked a lot like a younger version of Edward.

"Oh my goodness, look at you three. You just keep growing don't you?" Priscilla said with a giggle as she hugged them.

"Hey Mom, what was the big up-set the other day? Why didn't you want me to bring Diane here from the airport? You said that you'd call me, but I didn't hear from you yesterday. It's okay – I mean, Diane got to go finish up her Christmas shopping, and we took advantage of catching up with each others' gossip, but I was a bit worried," Charlotte said.

Priscilla nonchalantly looked away and walked towards the kitchen. Charlotte, still expecting an answer, followed her. Priscilla said, "Oh Charlotte, it wasn't anything important, I was just looking for your sister. Your father had a surprise for Christine, but she just kind of disappeared. He was really excited to give it to her, so I was calling everyone to see if they had seen her."

"Oh well that explains it... I guess. So what did dad get her," Charlotte asked.

"After dinner, I'll show you. Come on everyone, lets gather around the table for dinner," Priscilla called.

As they all gathered around the table, Christine came walking into the room. She tried to smile, and look happy. "Hi everyone," she said. She walked over to her place at the table, between Diane and her Mother.

"Let's sit," Priscilla said. "Edward, would you say a blessing."

"Could everyone please bow their heads?" Edward asked. "Dear Heavenly Father, Bless each and every one of us at this table. Please grace us with joy and peace throughout the coming year. We thank you Father for all you have given to us and we ask that you touch our hearts with understanding and forgiveness to those who have done wrong against us. Please be with us all and keep us safe as we venture out into the world this coming year. Bless this food we are about to eat. We thank you Lord, for providing it for us. In our Fathers' name, Amen."

Everyone in unison said, "Amen."

Charlotte began passing the wonderful food and helped her children with their plates.

"Which way are we passing?" Peter asked with a chuckle, as there seemed to be a plate traffic jam happening.

"Pass to the right," Edward said and they all started laughing. There wasn't a whole lot of talking going on during the meal, so the soft sounds of Bing Crosby Christmas carols could still be heard playing in the background, even over the clanking of silverware on their plates. It was a joyful holiday for most at the table. Christine was doing a relatively good job hiding her pain. She even made a few jokes with her niece and nephews. Diane told a few stories of schooling in Paris. The conversations were light, and a nice break from the darkness that loomed-over head.

After dinner, the ladies cleared the table and did the dishes. The kids sat in front of the fireplace waiting for the approval from their grandparents to tear into their gifts. They anxiously crawled around the tree looking at the gift tags for their names. Peter and

Edward were sitting on the sofa watching the kids. "They are really getting big Peter. How are Scott and Katie doing in school?" Edward asked.

"Well, the teacher says that Scott is a terrific student, and he seems to be a bit ahead of the other kids in his grade. Katie is doing good too. She has a lot of friends, and I think she likes art the best. I wonder where she gets that from," Peter said with a laugh. "I think that when Timothy starts school it will make it a lot easier for Charlotte. She really wants to put more effort into her paintings, but with the little one at home, it's hard for her to get focused."

Edward smiled and nodded his head in agreement. Just then the ladies came out of the kitchen with some coffee on a silver tray for the adults, and some hot chocolate for the kids. Diane sat the tray down on the coffee table and said, "Hey, so do any of you kids want some hot cocoa?" They stood up and ran over to Diane. "So, what about you Christine? You're still a kid," she said jokingly. Christine just smiled.

Charlotte butted in, "You kids be careful not to spill on Grandmas' carpet."

"Okay, who wants to open gifts?" asked Priscilla.

The kids all yelled in unison, "We do! We do!"

Priscilla sat on the floor next to the kids. Charlotte sat next to Peter on the sofa with Diane. Edward sat in his recliner, and Christine sat on the love seat by herself. Priscilla played Santa and gave the children all of their gifts, one at a time. They opened them all, and were overjoyed with their new toys. Then she gave Charlotte and Peter their gifts and Diane hers. Charlotte passed out her gifts to her parents, then to Diane and then Christine, then Diane handed out her gifts. After all the gifts had been opened, Edward asked, "Did anyone say dessert?"

"I heard something about that too," Peter chimed in.

"Okay, I get the hint," laughed Priscilla.

"I'll get it Mom," Christine said. She walked into the kitchen and gathered some plates and silverware.

She could hear Charlotte and her parents talking in the other room. "So what did you guys get Christine? Mom said that you were really excited to give her something, so I thought it must have been her Christmas gift. I noticed that you didn't give her anything tonight, so it must be big," Charlotte said.

"Edward, why don't you go show them and I'll help Christine in the kitchen," Priscilla said. Edward, Charlotte, Peter and Diane walked out to the garage. Edward opened the door, and there sat the yellow convertible VW Bug, that had gone pretty much by the wayside in light of the events that took place the day it was purchased. Edward had parked it in the garage that night, and it sat there without being admired by Christine.

As they went back into the house, they were all commenting on what a great gift it was, and how excited Christine must have been when they gave it to her. "I'm surprised that you stayed home tonight Christine. I would have thought that you'd be cruising all around the town with your new car," Diane said.

"Yeah, it's really cool. I love it," Christine answered. What she really wanted to say was, *If I could, I would get into my car, go get Jason and drive away!* As Christine took the plates to the table, Priscilla set the pies down and began to ask what kind everyone wanted. They all went in and sat at the table. Everyone was speaking at the same time, yelling out flavors. Priscilla just laughed.

Christine slipped away from the room without anyone noticing. She went into her parents' room. She sat down on their bed and looked at the phone. *Jason said that he would call. Why hadn't he called?* Christine began to reach for the phone. She picked it up and began to dial. Just as she finished the number, her mother called for her. She quickly hung up the phone and ran into the dining room.

"Where were you? I wanted to know what kind of pie you wanted," Priscilla said.

"Apple please, Mom. Thank you," Christine answered. She sat there, eating with everyone, trying her best to hold it together. She was choking back her tears, looking at her sisters, then at her parents. Then she looked at her nephews and her niece. Suddenly, she just wanted to be alone. Not even pie could hide her pain.

The evening was winding down and Christine helped the kids pack up all of their new toys. Priscilla and Edward said good-bye to Charlotte and Peter. "Diane, are you coming back with us or are you going to stay here?" Charlotte asked.

"I'll stay here. I wanted to show dad some pictures of my paintings, and I thought that mom and I could go shopping or something before I have to go back," Diane answered.

"Okay, we'll see you later then. Have a good time," Charlotte said as she hugged everyone and walked out the door. Christine told everyone good night and she went into her room and closed the door.

The next morning Diane and Priscilla made a big breakfast. They all sat at the table and ate. Christine didn't say much. Diane was talking about all of the interesting people she had met in Paris and about all the talented artist in her class. Edward was hanging on every word. When they were done eating, Christine asked, "Do you think that I could take my car out for a spin over to Jane's house, so I can show her my cool ride?"

Priscilla and Edward looked at each other with raised eyebrows. "She is probably busy with her family Christine, why don't you wait," Priscilla said.

Diane and Edward went into his art studio, which was one of the bedrooms that he had converted. Edward wanted to show her some of the paintings he had been working on. Christine watched TV for most of the day, and it seemed like everyone was moving in fast motion around her. The phone rang. Christine's heart dropped to her feet. She went running into the kitchen, but was instantly disappointed to see that her mother was on it. "I don't know Charlotte," she said, "Let me go look," as she set the phone down and walked into the other room to look for a lost toy.

Christine went back into the den to watch TV. Why hadn't Jason called? *This is ridiculous*, she thought. *Where could he be?* All kinds of thoughts raced through her head, and then she stopped. She had a thought that made her sick. Her face got hot, then she started sweating. She got goose bumps all over her arms, but not the good kind. *His father! He must have told his father.*

The next day, Edward went off to work. Priscilla and Diane went shopping and out to lunch. Priscilla took the VW keys and put them in her purse before she left. Christine searched all over her parents' room for the keys. She went into the studio and searched through all of the drawers in the desk. She looked through all of the little cubby holes that held paint and brushes. She was so frustrated. She gave up and went into her room to listen to music. She flipped through the channels bouncing from song to song. It seemed like her mother had been gone such a long time. She looked at the clock. Her father would be home in about an hour to take Diane back over to Charlotte's house. She and Peter were going to take Diane to the airport the next morning. Just as she got up from her bed and looked out of the window for what felt like the hundredth time, her mother and Diane pulled up. They were carrying in grocery bags. Christine went outside to help them. Diane had taken a few bags into the house and Christine was grabbing the last of the bags. "Why did you take my car keys Mom?" she asked.

"Your father and I don't want you going anywhere right now.

You act rash, you don't think things through... you're just too un-
predictable right now. We are worried about you, and this is all so
new. We just feel that it would be better for you, not to have the
freedom to go make any more poor decisions until we get a chance
to figure this whole mess out and..."

Priscilla was in mid-sentence when Christine cut her off and
said, "Oh, I see! Thanks. Thanks a hell of a lot! You're gonna treat
me like a baby now," and she stormed into the house.

Meanwhile, Edward was turning off the lights in his office.
Things were pretty slow from the holiday, and he really didn't have
much to do. As he put some papers into his desk drawer, he heard
a door shut, way off in the distance. He frowned. He got up and
walked over to one of the office doors to look out at the rest of
the building. There was nobody there. None of the lights were on
in the adjoining office. He turned around, and there, sitting in a
chair in front of his desk was Mr. Hushinson. He had a cigarette in
his hand and he was puffing away. "Mr. McMillan?" he asked.

"Yes, and who are you?" Edward asked.

"My name is not important, however, the reason I'm here, is.
Due to the nature of a current 'problem' and the humiliation that
'it' could result to both families, I've been asked to help facilitate a
discrete intervention to solve this 'problem.' It needs to be ad-
dressed in a rapid fashion."

Edward walked back over to his desk and sat down. "Go ahead,
I'm listening" he said.

"I have been asked to come and speak to you. Do you understand the extremely delicate nature of this predicament," Mr.
Hushinson asked.

"Yes, I do. But do you also know that my daughter is sixteen,
and this little 'predicament' as you call it, could land someone's
son in jail? Or at the minimum, paint him out as sleazy womanizer
like his father? Taking advantage of an underage girl?" Edward

asked.

Mr. Hushinson, put out his cigarette on the floor. He sat forward on his chair and put one elbow on the desk as he said, "Look Mr. McMillan, nobody's going to jail. You'd have a pretty hard time proving that. Your idle threats are nothing more that puffery. You have just as much at stake and you know it. You don't want this to get out anymore than we do. The less messy this gets, the better for all of us. Get my drift? We think that the best way to resolve this issue, is for your daughter to abort the problem."

"Let me get this straight. You want my daughter to do what? My sixteen year old daughter? Have an abortion? Are you insane? I am not going to make her do that!" Edward stood up, leaned forward and put his hands on the desk. "There is no telling what could happen to her. The nerve of that guy! Who the hell does he think he is, ordering me to abort the 'problem' that his son created," Edward said as he shook is head in disgust.

"I said that it would be the best. The cleanest," Mr. Hushinson said as he took his elbow off the desk and sat back in the chair.

"Absolutely not! We do not condone those actions under any circumstance. It's murder! The fact that you think that's even a viable option shows the true 'character' of that family."
Edward grew more and more heated. "You can tell that son of a..."

Mr. Hushinson interrupted Edward, "Well, we do have another option. But let me just tell you, it's one or the other. We are not going to negotiate any further. Do you know the power behind the man? Do you think that for one minute he's going to let something like this ruin his reputation? Here's the deal – she either gets an abortion, or your family moves away. Completely disappears. No traces here at all. After the birth, that child will be given away. No one can know to whom this child is related. Do you understand Edward? To help facilitate this, we are prepared to offer you a small house in the mountains, to relocate you and your family, and a cash settlement."

Edward could feel his face getting hot, and his heart pounding in his chest as he said, "You think you can just buy us off like that? Erase us basically? I have a career here at the studio. My daughter is still in school. My wife has her clubs and social engagements. Our church groups... We aren't just going to change our whole lives for HIM. After all, has he forgotten HIS son got my daughter pregnant?"

Mr. Hushinson stood up and leaned into the desk putting his face up close to Edwards.

"Your career?" Hushinson said in a low cold tone. He let out a little laugh, "Your career is OVER! You can either put in for an early retirement on your own, or we can do it for you, it's up to you. You WILL move away, and you WILL take your family and disappear. This is not negotiable Edward. I guess you haven't figured that out yet. You have no power in this situation. I'm trying to help you make the best and simplest decision here, and you think you can make demands? You think you can throw your weight around like some big shot? Who's to say your daughter didn't set this entire thing up? Entrapment? Lied about her age? There are plenty of scenarios that will 'paint a picture' that will fuck your 'clean-cut' religious little world up for good. Get my drift there Edward? You ever breathe a word to anyone about this, and any deal made, is off. This is never mentioned again. Your family tells no one, and nobody gets hurt. Don't think that your two aspiring art-ist daughters are safe either. They could meet an untimely retirement before they even get started. If this is ever mentioned, if it ever mysteriously becomes public, we will take other measures to ensure you and your entire family get what's coming to you." Hushinson grabbed his coat. "I'll let you think about it, and I'll be back tomorrow to finalize the details. Be a smart man Edward. I'd hate to see something bad happen." With that said, he left the room and vanished into the darkness of the night.

Edward drove home completely shaken. Unsure how this was all going to play out. He didn't want to move, and there was no option for an abortion. Coming from an extremely religious upbringing himself, and carrying on that tradition with his own family... even just the thought repulsed him.

Diane and Priscilla were in the kitchen just finishing up dinner as Edward walked through the door. Priscilla looked at Edward and she knew that he was worried. Something terrible must have happened. They ate dinner, trying to keep the conversation light and let Diane do most of the talking. When they finished dinner, Diane and Priscilla went into the kitchen to wash the dishes.

"Mom, is everything okay? Dad seems preoccupied with something. He barely spoke at dinner. Are you guys having problems?"

"Oh he's fine, he's probably just tired. Don't worry about it," Priscilla said as she looked at the clock. "Look at the time. It's getting late, I think that we should get you over to Charlotte's house."

Edward and Priscilla drove Diane over to Charlotte's. As Edward drove, Priscilla told Diane to keep in touch with them. "You don't call very often, and it's nice to hear what you are doing from time to time." Priscilla turned to look at Diane in the back seat and smiled.

When they pulled up in front of Charlotte's house Diane asked, "Aren't you coming in?"

"No, sweetie, I have a few things that I really need to take care of tonight, that can't wait until tomorrow," Priscilla said as she hugged her.

"Have a safe flight honey and call us when you get in," Edward said.

They said their good-byes and were on their way back home. Priscilla didn't ask Edward what was wrong. They drove all the way home without a single word. When they got home, Edward took

Priscilla into their bedroom. Edward closed the door, but not quite all the way. "I had a visitor at my office today. He told me that 'they' want Christine to get an abortion. He pretty much demand-ed it," Edward said with a crack in his voice.

Christine's room was across from theirs, so she heard every-thing. She sat on the floor, in back of her door, so if her parents looked, they wouldn't see her eavesdropping. Her eyes filled up with tears. Little did she know that her father had left the door slightly open on purpose, so she could hear. "An abortion?" Priscil-la asked. *What are they thinking? I know people opt to do that, but I've heard they are dangerous too. Why does he think he can make decisions like this for OUR daughter? How on earth could they be so insensitive to...*"

Edward stopped her. "I told him that it's not an option."

Priscilla, still shocked said, "Edward, what are our options? This is all getting so convoluted. They aren't even thinking about Christine. I mean, don't they understand that she's going to have to drop out of school, and the emotional upheaval she is going to experience?" Christine just sat there, shaking her head, listening to her parents plan out her life. *No one asked me what I want,* she thought.

As she sat there listening to her parents, she started getting angry. *No one mentioned Jason's name in all of this. Could he pos-sibly be in agreement to all of this? How could he be so cold after everything they had said to each other?* She couldn't stand it any longer so she got up, closed her door and turned up her music.

Edward walked over to their door and shut it completely. "I left the door open a little bit because I wanted Christine to hear us. I want her to get angry. Maybe she'll lose her interest in that boy if she hears what they want her to do. Now, here's the other part that I don't want Christine to know about. We have another option, but she can never find out about it. She has to think that we did this all on our own. She has to build up a resentment for that boy, so she freely agrees to this too. Now, don't interrupt me and just hear me out. We were offered a home in the Mountains, and a cash settlement. I assume the cash is for the doctor visits, the hospital, and some getting started over money. Do you understand that this situation could put us on easy street? That man has a lot of money. If we play our cards right, we'll never have to worry about money again. He didn't tell me how much exactly, but I understand that they just want to get rid of us as soon as possible. He told me that we can't tell anyone. Ever. If we do, he'll make sure that I suffer, you suffer, and the girls suffer. Even Charlotte and Diane will suffer. He said they would never become artists."

Priscilla asked, "Are you telling me that we have to move away?"

"Yes and no. I think I know how to make this work, for everyone. You are going to have to trust me. I know how to work this, but I don't want to tell you everything now. The man that came to my office is going to come back to my office tomorrow, and I'll talk to him. I think that we need to tell Christine a very small amount, but we do need to tell her how badly they are trying to get rid of that baby. My idea is, that if she believes that boy abandon her, she'll hate him so much, she'll gladly give up the baby. Why would she want that constant reminder in her life? We certainly don't want to raise it, and I certainly don't want to look at it day in and day out, knowing the evil people it's related to! So, do you trust me? Do you agree to go along with whatever I say, without questioning me?" She hesitantly agreed.

Edward called Christine into their room. "Christine, can you please turn that awful music off and come in here?

"What is it now," sighed Christine.

Edward continued speaking. "We have a new situation that came up today, and we need to talk about it. We have a big problem, and I'm trying to handle it. Your boyfriend's father is making my life a living hell. I am trying to make the best decisions for our family. You can not, I repeat, can not tell anyone about this situation between you and Jason. None of your friends, no teachers, not even your sisters. No one can find out, that you two had any kind of relationship at all. All you have to do is listen to your mother and I. You do exactly what we tell you with no questions. Do you understand me?"

"Okay, so I can't tell anyone about him, but can I at least talk to Jason," Christine asked as her eyes filled with tears.

"No Christine, you have to forget Jason. His family has him protected, and they will not allow him to contact you. You cannot contact him either. I can't begin to tell you the problems it will cause if you do contact him. He's dead to you," Edward said. "I know this is hard for you, and you're emotional but you'll get over this in time. I promise you will not hurt like this forever. It's just a part of life and making mistakes."

Christine ran back to her room, crawled into her bed, sobbing and fell asleep.

The next day, Edward waited for the mystery man to appear in his office just as he had done the day before. It was 6:00 pm, and everyone had gone home. Edward turned off the lights, and walked to his car. A black Cadillac was sitting beside Edward's car. As he walked up to his car, the back window of the Cadillac rolled down a few inches. "Get in Edward," said a voice from the back seat.

Edward couldn't quite make out the voice, so he hesitated a bit before walking closer. The rear windows were completely blacked out so he couldn't see inside.

Mr. Hushinson rolled the window down a little more and made the request again. "Get in Edward. I have the package we discussed yesterday. Just get in the car, so we can finish this," Hushinson snapped.

Edward slowly reached for the handle of the Cadillac. As he opened the door he could see Hushinson, with a briefcase in his lap. Edward got in and closed the door and Hushinson rolled the window back up for privacy.

Edward thought he'd get the first words in. "Before we discuss any of the demands you made yesterday, I want to tell you that I think that Mr. Davis is a low life. He's a real piece of work, that guy. With all his power, and prestige, to just push people around, he's really just a son of a bitch, a damn bully," Edward barked.

"I'm not here to make you like him, I'm here to make sure that you understand how devastating this could be for your family if you don't cooperate," Hushinson said coldly.

"My wife and I talked last night. This is the deal. As I told you yesterday, abortion is not an option for my daughter. Trust me, we don't want any ties to the Davis family. Probably even more than they don't want the tie to ours. We will move away – when we feel the time is right. Not when you tell us to. This is my daughter's life, damn it! You have no right to treat her or us this way," Edward said assertively.

"I don't give a shit about your rights. My job is to make you disappear. I will be watching you and your family, until the child is gone. If you renege on your part of the bargain, we will destroy you, plain and simple," Hushinson's promised.

Realizing it was futile to argue with Mr. Hushinson's unrelenting overpowering nature, Edward reluctantly agreed to the terms. Mr. Hushinson drafted up an agreement, with time frames for the cabin transfer, as well as the promised cash payoff.

"Alright, then we are in agreement with the terms of the contract. That you will put your house up for sale, and the story is that you decided to retire early and travel. That within a few months, you will receive an envelope and inside will be a key to a safe deposit box. The deed, and the cash will be inside the box.

Once you have cleared out the safe deposit box, and I can verify that the child is gone, our relationship is over – unless..."

"Yeah, I got it!" Edward snapped. Edward and Hushinson got out of the car. Hushinson got into the front seat of the Cadillac, and sped away. Somehow Edward felt that he had just sold his soul to the devil.

CHAPTER SEVEN

Winter vacation was over. Christine had to go back to school. She pulled up in the school parking lot and parked next to a few of her friends. They all had stories to tell about their Christmas vacation. Some of them had gone skiing, some of them visited family out of state, and a few of them had met new boys, which was the ultimate trump card of holiday tales. They were all overly bubbly and excited for each others' adventurous tales. She listened to them laugh and laugh. "So what did you do Christine?" one of the girls asked.

"Not a lot, just hung out with my family mostly. My sister came in from Paris. I haven't seen her in a long time, so that was cool." The girls just looked at Christine, who seemed less than enthusiastic about her vacation time. "I did get this car for Christmas though," Christine said as she turned slightly and pointed to her new car.

They just looked at her with blank faces. Christine turned back to them and noticed they were just staring at her. *Was there something on her shirt? Did she have something on her face? Did she look different? Oh my gosh, did they know?* It finally occurred to Christine, that they must have thought she was bragging or something, to say she got a car like it was nothing special. Along with being kind of stand offish like she was, she probably came across stuck up and bitchy to them. Christine smiled and said, "It sounds like you guys had a much better time than I did." They smiled at her, and continued to talk among themselves. Christine just turned and walked away.

Christine went to her classes as usual. She walked through the halls which felt like she was walking in slow motion, and everyone else around her was moving extra fast. For weeks, she did the same thing. She went to her classes, counted the minutes until school was over and then went home. One day after school, Jane saw Christine as Christine was walking through the school parking lot. "Hey Christine," she called. Christine turned around.

"Hi Jane, I haven't seen you in a long time, where have you been?" Christine asked. The girls hugged.

"Oh, they put me in the Honor's program, so I've been really busy with the schoolwork. I know I haven't been able to spend any time with you lately, and I'm sorry. My dad is really pushing me to keep my grades up so I can get into an Ivy league college, and become an attorney like him. He was so happy to hear it, he took my whole family to Hawaii for a three-day weekend celebration. I see you got a new ride. Very cool Christine," Jane replied.

Christine wanted to tell Jane everything she had been through, and everything she was going through. Instead, Christine said, "Yeah, it gets me around. I'm so happy for you though. You really deserve it Jane."

They talked for a little while then Christine told her that she had to get home. "I need to help my old lady do some things around the house. I haven't been doing so hot in school lately and she said that if I didn't do some extra junk for her, she was gonna take my car away."

"Oh that's a bummer," Jane said. "Well I guess I'll see you around. Don't be a stranger. Maybe we can get together soon and go to the movies or something, okay?"

"Sure, that sounds groovy," Christine said. She continued walking towards her car, hopped in and drove home.

Priscilla was in the kitchen making cookies. "I was starting to worry Christine, you are a little late," she said.

"Mom, I just stopped to talk to Jane for a few minutes. I haven't seen her for months. I think the last time I saw her was before winter break. She told me that she made the Honor's program at school, and her dad was so happy, he took the whole family to Hawaii," Christine said.

"Well good for her. She's a good girl. You should have spent more time hanging out with her. Maybe you wouldn't have ruined your life," Priscilla said.

"Look Mom, I know that you hate me. I know that I made a mistake. I'm sorry. I can't take it back." Christine started to cry. "Why don't you try to look at it from my side for a change? Everyone is planning my life for me. I don't have a life anymore. Do you think that I did this on purpose?" she asked.

"No, I don't think you did this on purpose, but you made the wrong decision. A decision that has altered MY life, not to mention your father's too. He worked hard his whole life to provide for you and your sisters, to have it all ripped away from him by a poor decision YOU made," Priscilla yelled.

Christine ran to her room crying. She flopped onto her bed sobbing uncontrollably.

Priscilla continued to make her cookies. She felt bad for yelling at Christine, but she felt that she needed to make sure Christine realized just how many sacrifices they were having to make because of her life changing choice. About an hour later, Priscilla went into Christine's bedroom with a few cookies on a plate. "Christine?" she said. "I'm sorry I yelled at you. I know this is hard on you too. It's just...," she set the cookies on the night stand, "We have to move away from everything we know. I have to leave all of my friends behind. We've lived in this house for twenty-eight years. All of my memories of you girls growing up, are in this house..."

Christine sat up and wiped away her tears and said, "Do you understand how alone I feel, Mom? I have to leave everything I know too. I didn't think that my life would be ending like this," Christine sobbed.

"Christine, your life isn't ending. You just have to start over when this is all done," Priscilla said as she put her hand on Christine's shoulder.

Edward walked into the room. "What's going on in here?" he asked as he walked over to a chair in the corner of Christine's room and sat down.

"I was just telling Christine that her life isn't over," answered Priscilla.

"How am I supposed to finish school, or get a job, or – anything, with a baby?" Christine asked.

"What do you mean with a baby?" asked Edward.

"Let me handle this Edward," Priscilla said. "Christine, your father and I were talking... I don't think you understand. I mean your life isn't over, you can start over after you have the baby. You aren't going to keep it, you are going to put it up for adoption. Your father and I are going to be with you, we are going to see you through this, but we aren't going to raise your child with you. We don't want any reminders of that family. They are horrible people. Why would you want to keep a baby that is just going to remind you of how horrible they were," Priscilla asked.

"I don't care about that. This is my baby too. I can't just give it away to some stranger," Christine yelled as she was growing more and more upset. "Oh forget it, you just don't understand. You are so tied up in your own world Mom, you can't see what this is doing to me. Just leave me alone please." Silently crying, Christine flopped her body back down on her bed and rolled over to turn her back to her parents .

Edward and Priscilla walked out of the room. Christine stayed in her room the rest of the night. She turned on the radio, mindlessly twisting the knob, scanning the channels. She paused when she heard a tune that caught her ear. The station was playing some new kind of music that she'd never heard before. It seemed to fit her mood perfectly. It was depressing and dark sounding. She never listened to music like this. She normally liked to listen to bands like the Beatles, Sonny and Cher, the Monkees and the Beach Boys. The song was titled 'The End' and it was by the Doors. This was a new dramatic sound, but then again, everything in Christine's life was new and dramatic.

The next day, Christine went to the record store after school and bought the Doors single of that new song she heard. When she walked out of the store to get into her car she looked out towards the street as a car caught her eye. There was Jason, sitting at the stop light. She just stood there, her stomach was all tied in knots and her eyes filled up with tears.

Just as she turned to get into her car, Jason saw her. *Oh my God. I don't believe it,* he thought. *What should I do? Do I follow her? Do I turn around? Why is this light still red?!*

Christine backed out of her parking space and drove to the exit. Jason was still staring at her, but she wasn't looking his way. The light had now changed for Jason, and someone honked at him. As he drove past the driveway where Christine was waiting to exit, they locked eyes. He could see the tears rolling down Christine's cheeks.

Her heart was pounding and she could barely swallow. Jason wanted to pull over, but he didn't. He kept driving and Christine lost sight of him as the cars kept streaming behind Jason's.

Finally, Christine was able to pull out of the driveway. She turned up her stereo as loud as she could and drove home. She went into her bedroom and put on the new single she just bought. Priscilla hated the music. Every time she walked by Christine's room she would open her door and tell her to turn it off. Christine would only turn it up louder.

Jason went over to his father's house. He walked into the library where his father was sitting, looking at a script. "What's going on Jason?" he said, annoyed.

"It's just... I just saw... her," Jason said nervously.

"I told you boy, you can never talk to her again. I don't care if you see her everyday. It's over. She doesn't exist. I handled the problem, and that's all there is to it," Keith said loudly.

"I know Dad, I didn't even want to tell you, it's just that I didn't get to say good-bye to her. I didn't get to tell her that I was sorry that this all happened. You stepped in and it just all happened so fast. I go to school, and I try not to think about it, about her, about any of this. I was doing pretty good until today. Please Dad, just let me call her. I need to say..."

"You don't need to say shit boy. I've said it for you, and this is the last conversation we're having about it. If you want me to let you pay for your own schooling, and cut you off from the family, keep it up. I have enough crap going on, I don't need any more from you," Keith snapped as he got up and stormed out of the room.

Erin heard the commotion and came into the room. "You know I love you, just as if you were one of my own children, and I hate to see you in so much pain. I'm sorry he talked to you like that Jason. He's really been under a lot of pressure lately. The little ones seem to be more demanding and need more attention from him, and we had a little argument last night because he is going away again for a few months to shoot a film. Just give him some time. This will all be a memory someday. I know it seems like the end of the world, but it isn't." Erin kissed him on the head and she walked out of the room. Jason sat there for a few minutes and then got up and walked out of the house.

He stood on the front porch and stared off into the distance. *Poor Christine,* he thought. *This is all my fault, and I can't do anything to help her.* He slowly walked down the steps and got into his car and drove away. Keith watched him drive away from his bedroom window and he got on the phone. "Dan, it's Keith. Find out what that "Hush" guy needs to get that family out of here now! I want it done by the weekend. I have to leave for a few months, and I don't want this hanging over my head."

Dan was at his office. He wasn't expecting such trepidation from Keith, *something must have shaken him*, he thought. "Keith, it will take a week or so alone, just to get everything together. I still need you to send me over the money. In the meantime, I'll send you over the deed to the property. You and Erin need to sign it, get it notarized and send it back, then that part is as good as done. As far as them moving out of here that soon, I highly doubt they'll pull their daughter out of school so close to the end of the year. It would look suspicious. It's just not freezable, but I'll let 'Hush' know the urgency for their relocation, and see what he can do," Dan said.

"Fine just do it, but I want a firm date," Keith barked and he hung up the phone.

A few weeks later, Edward came home from work early. Priscilla was ironing some clothes in the den. Edward walked up and gave her a kiss. "Look what came to the office today." He held up a large yellow envelope. "There was a key in the envelope to a safe deposit box, and a note inside. Edward read the last part out loud to Priscilla. "We feel that you are not taking the situation seriously. Your home still isn't listed for sale. Christine may start to show signs of being pregnant soon. We need to finalize this portion of our agreement, so you need to make the arrangements for the move." Edward shook his head and said, "I can't believe that they are still watching us. They make me sick. I think that you need to take Christine shopping and get her some less contoured clothes. I also think that it's about time to start thinking about selling the house. I called a realtor today after I got this package, she'll be here tomorrow. If they are watching us, it will only be a matter of time before they do something else more drastic. I don't want anything we do, to be on their time frame. I'll go by the safe deposit box in the morning and clear it out."

Priscilla stopped ironing and looked up at Edward. "So this is it?" she asked. "It's really come down to selling the house and moving away? The time just kind of flew by, or maybe I was pretending that nothing was really going on. Either way, it doesn't make me feel any better." Priscilla began to iron again. "You know Edward, I really need to take Christine to the doctor before we move, just to make sure that everything is okay. We need to figure out how this adoption thing works, and get everything organized so we can carry on after Christine gives birth," Priscilla said.

"Well make the appointment then. Find a place out of the area, maybe towards Los Angeles. I'll take a day off from work, if you can get an appointment and we'll all go together. You can tell Christine that she is going to have to miss school that day," Edward said as he walked over to Priscilla and squeezed her shoulder.

The next day the realtor stopped by the house. Christine answered the door. A woman wearing a buttoned up, black and white plaid jacket and matching tweed skirt, was standing there. Her short red, extra large bouffant styled hair, caught her off guard. She had to keep herself from laughing.

"Yes, can I help you?" Christine asked.

"Hello dear, my name is Dolores Feldman, I have an appointment with your parents. Are they home?" she asked.

"Sure, come on in," Christine said. She showed Dolores to the living room, and told her to have a seat.

Edward and Priscilla were in their bedroom looking at the package that Edward had picked up from the safe deposit box. There was the deed to the cabin in Lake Arrowhead, and $150,000 in cash inside. "What a jerk," Priscilla said, "It must be nice to just pay people off to get them out of your life."

"Some people just operate that way. Maybe that's how he's gotten so far in his life," Edward said.

"Well I guess that it's better this way. I bet the apple doesn't fall far from the tree. Could you imagine if we had to deal with them for the rest of our lives?" Priscilla asked.

"No way! I would just love to tell him where to go," Edward said.

"You know, it's just as much his fault for not taking responsibility for his kid. He needs to suffer a bit. We sure are! I hope that parting with $150,000 brings him pain," said Priscilla.

Edward grabbed the stack of money and put it in a small metal lock box in his closet. "This money is going to help us start over, and I don't feel bad about taking it from him at all, and frankly, we should have demanded more," Edward said.

Just then, Christine went into her parents' room and told them that there was a lady there to see them. "Here we go Edward," Priscilla said.

They walked into the living room and sat down. They talked to Dolores and then they showed her around the house. Christine was in her room listening to music when the door opened. "This is our daughters' room," Priscilla said. She looked at Christine with squinted eyes, which she knew meant to turn off the music.

Dolores looked around and said, "This is nice, and where are you moving to?" as they walked out of the room.

Christine got up off her bed and walked over to the door and shut it. She pressed her ear up to the door to see if she could make out what they were saying.

"Oh my husband is retiring and we thought that we needed a change. Our family is smaller now, and we don't need so much space." Their voices got fainter as they walked away. They all sat down at the dining room table. Dolores started writing up the papers to list their home. Priscilla found it hard to keep from crying. She excused herself and went into the kitchen to get some drinks.

When she came back into the room, they were ready to sign the papers. She set the tray of drinks down, passed the glasses around and picked up a pen. "Where do I sign?" Priscilla asked.

"Right next to all of mine dear," Edward replied.

"I'll have a sign put up in the morning, and if there is anything else you need, just call my office," Dolores said. They walked her to the front door and then shook hands and said goodbye.

Priscilla turned to Edward and somberly said, "I'll go get dinner started," as she walked towards the kitchen.

Edward went to his painting room and sat down. He just sat there, blankly staring out the window until he heard Priscilla call him and Christine for dinner. They sat at the table and ate. It was very quiet. Too quiet. Everyone just looking down at their plates, picking at their food.

Priscilla broke the silence by clearing her throat. "Christine, we are taking you to the doctor tomorrow. Your father and I want to make sure that everything is set up so we won't have to worry about anything when it comes time for you to deliver. The doctor is in Los Angeles, so you'll have to take the day off school," Priscilla said.

"Whatever. That's fine, I don't really want to go to school anymore anyway. I don't fit in. I can't talk to any of my friends, and I hate my teachers," Christine said, as she kept eating.

The next day they drove to the doctors' office. They pulled up to a plain looking, large white cement building. It didn't really look like a normal medical building. "What is this place?" Christine asked.

"It's a low-profile doctors' office that handles situations like ours. Don't worry, you'll be fine," Priscilla said.

They walked into one of the offices and Christine sat down next to Edward in a chair in the corner of the room. Priscilla checked Christine in, and the receptionist asked her to fill out some forms.

When Priscilla was done, she took the papers back up to the desk. Just then, a nurse poked her head out of the door." Christine McMillan," she called. Christine and Priscilla got up and walked over to the door. "Follow me," she said. They walked a short distance down the hallway and the nurse pointed into one of the rooms." Go in here and the doctor will be right in." She shut the door behind them.

Christine sat up on the exam table, and Priscilla sat in a chair. They waited about ten minutes and then the doctor knocked on the door. He walked into the room and set the chart down on the little counter. He was an older man in his late sixties, who had a bit of a pudgy belly. His hair was gray and he wore black-framed glasses. He looked like a 'kind-hearted-grandpa' type. "Hi Christine, my name is Dr. Newman. I have a few questions to ask you and then I want to do an exam." He asked Christine when her last period was and how she had been feeling in general. "I noticed that you haven't been seeing an obstetrician, so I am happy you're here now."

Christine said, "I went to the doctor around the end of December, and he told me that he thought I was due sometime in August. I was feeling tired, but that's gone now. I guess I feel fine."

Dr. Newman looked at Priscilla and said, "I have some other papers I need you and your husband to fill out. Could you take them out to the waiting room and when I am done with the exam, I'll come get you."

Priscilla stood up and grabbed the papers from the doctor. She took them to Edward in the waiting room. It was a small room with very few chairs for a traditional doctors' office. It had some homey touches, like plants here and there and magazines on the end tables that were between the chairs. They read through the packet of papers.

The doctor did an exam on Christine, took some blood for some tests, and listened to the baby's heartbeat. "Everything sounds good. Your blood pressure is fine," he said as he looked at her chart comparing the notes with his exam. "Let's see, you weighed 118 lbs. before you got pregnant. Lets see how much you weigh now, come step on the scale for me."

Christine hopped off the table and stood on the scale. "It looks like you have gained about six pounds. Let me see, you are due in August, and it's April 20th. Hum, I think that you are right about on target for weight. You know, this is the point that the baby will really start putting weight on. You need to be very careful from now on. You don't want to gain too much. It'll be harder for you to lose the weight after the baby's born. Do you have any questions for me Christine?" he asked.

"Nope, not really," Christine answered.

"Okay then, let me go see if your mom is done with the papers." He leaned out into the hallway and asked the nurse to go call Priscilla and Edward to come in.

Priscilla and Edward had finished filling out the papers and were looking them over. The nurse went out to the waiting room to get Priscilla and Edward. She looked at them and said, "The doctor is ready, you can both come in now."

They walked into the room and sat down. "We filled out as much as we could, but some of this information we don't know," Edward said.

"Don't worry about it, it's all preliminary. The social worker will fill out the rest, and before we finalize any of this, you'll have to talk to her. It will be towards the end of the pregnancy, so don't worry about it for now. I will send them the file. They are in our building, so the next time I see Christine, I will have an appointment set up for you to meet with the social worker."

They shook the doctors hand and left.

"What was that all about," Christine asked.

"Just some forms that we have to fill out for the delivery and stuff. Nothing that you need to concern yourself about right now. Let's go get some lunch, and go home," Edward said.

Christine just rolled her eyes, shook her head and whispered to herself, "Always the last to know, kept in the dark, letting everyone else run my life. This sucks."

CHAPTER EIGHT

It was the beginning of May, and it was Christine's seventeenth birthday. Charlotte stopped by the house to drop off a gift for her. As she went into the house, she saw her mom frosting a cake in the kitchen. "Hey Mom," Charlotte said as she walked up and gave her a kiss. "I still can't believe that you are selling the house. You didn't really even tell me why. I mean it's all just such a big surprise."

"Well your father thought it's time to downsize a bit. He also thought it would be fun to travel this summer, then next year he could just relax and start painting again. He has worked so hard for our family, I think it's time he did something for himself, don't you?" Priscilla asked.

"Yes Mom, I do. I think it's great. But the timing just seemed strange, with Christine heading into her senior year next year and all. Well, maybe it will help Christine too, you know, traveling with just the two of you, maybe it will make her feel special. Has she snapped out of whatever she was going through at Christmas?" Charlotte asked.

"Yes, I think she's fine now, nothing to worry about. It was probably just a phase," Priscilla said.

"Hey what's going on in here?" Christine asked as she walked into the house.

"Hey, it's my little sister, Happy Birthday. Long time, no see. You're getting old now. Ah, and it looks like you've put on a little weight too! Look at you, your face is a little puffy and your cheeks are all rosy," Charlotte said as she took a closer look at Christine.

"Oh stop it, Charlotte, Christine looks fine. She was a bit too thin. I thought that she needed to gain a little weight. I didn't think that she was looking healthy," Priscilla said and then she quickly changed the subject.

Just then, the phone rang. Christine answered it. "Mom, it's Dolores," Christine said, as she handed the phone to her mom.

"Hi Priscilla, I have an offer I need to show you, I think you will both be very happy," said Dolores.

Priscilla said, "Stop by this evening. Edward will be home from work by then." Priscilla hung up the phone. "That was the realtor, she has an offer for our house. She is going to come over tonight and tell us what it is."

"Well, I wish we could have stayed for dinner tonight, but Scott and Tim have the flu. I should get home to help Peter. Mom, call me and let me know what happens tonight. Christine, Happy Birthday. You know we all love you, and hope that you have a great seventeenth year. Stop by sometime and hang out with us this summer." Charlotte kissed Christine on the forehead and gave her a big hug.

Priscilla walked her to the door. "I'll call you later. Say hi to Peter and the kids."

When Edward got home, Priscilla told him that Dolores would be presenting an offer. "She said that we'd be happy. I have such mixed feelings," she sighed.

"I hope that it's a short escrow, I put in for my retirement today," Edward quipped.

"Oh Edward, I'm sorry, that must have been so hard for you," Priscilla said.

"Well, it came as a shock to a few of the guys, but I just told them that it was time for me to relax. I wanted to put more effort into painting, and do some traveling with you. I made it kind of a joke. I said that the old man should move over and let some of the youngsters have a crack," Edward said with a smile.

Just then the doorbell rang. Priscilla went to open the door. "Hi Dolores. Please come in and have a seat, I'll get us some coffee."

Dolores pulled some papers out of her case and set them on the table. "I received these this morning, and the buyer is really anxious to find out what you think. I know that they love the house, and they have four children. They raved about the school district here," said Dolores.

Edward said, "We had one child when we bought this house, and then the other two girls came after. It's been a great family home for us. I am glad that someone else will love it as much as we have." Priscilla stood next to Edward and put her hand on his shoulder. Dolores told them about the offer, and they accepted.

The next few weeks were full of packing and tears. Priscilla was torn about leaving the home they had loved for so many years, and Christine was just plain torn. She didn't want to move away either. She would have moments of sorrow, but that would quickly turn to anger. She didn't think about Jason as much as she used to, but there were times when she couldn't help herself. Christine came home from school one afternoon, and saw her mother in the den packing some pictures.

Christine sat down on the floor and grabbed one of the photo albums and started flipping through the pages.

"Do you remember that vacation to Hawaii, Christine? We had such a good time, life seemed so much simpler back then. How old were you," Priscilla asked.

"I think I was about ten wasn't I?" Christine asked. Christine pointed to a picture on the page. "Oh here is a cute picture of Diane and Dad on the beach. I remember that day. Dad got sunburned, and Diane caught a bunch of sand crabs and put them on his back. Christine laughed. "Oh my gosh, Mom, feel my stomach."

Priscilla hesitated. "Christine, I don't really want to feel it move. I am having a hard enough time dealing with all of this. If I feel it moving in your stomach, it will just seem so much more real," Priscilla said.

"Please Mom," Christine asked again. Priscilla leaned forward and put her hand on Christine's stomach.

"Is this the first time you've felt anything Christine?" Priscilla asked.

"No, I've felt it move before, but this time it's a lot harder," Christine said.

"Wow, it really is kicking up a storm isn't it," Priscilla said.

Christine sat there on the floor for a few minutes, and then she looked at her mom. "Isn't there any way I could..." Christine stopped talking. "Never mind," she said. She got up and went into her room.

Priscilla waited for a few minutes and then she went into Christine's room. "Honey, I know that this is really difficult. Just try not to think about it. If you don't get too attached to it, it won't be so hard in the end."

"Mom, can you try to imagine giving one of us away? It's the same thing, only I'm not married. It is still a part of me, and it's even a part of you. I know that I made a mistake, but I have nightmares about giving the baby away... Like say, what if the people are mean and hurt the baby. What if they can't provide a good home? What if no one adopts it, and it has to live in a foster home? What if..."

Priscilla interrupted her. "Christine, they have to be screened. These people have to pass all kinds of testing about their backgrounds, their finances, their religion and all kinds of things. They are not just going to put the baby in a store for anyone to take. You know, you don't need all the stress in your condition. You are a young girl with your whole life ahead of you. You don't need to think about raising a child. You will start over with your life, you'll get married and you'll have children someday. Please just trust me on this," Priscilla said.

"Mom, I will never be the same. I don't think that it's right, to just get rid of a child like it was an animal or something," Christine said as she tried to hold back her tears.

"Pull yourself together! That's enough talk right now about this. We have a lot of things to do for the move, and you need to concentrate on your finals for school." Priscilla hugged Christine and left her room.

Christine had a lot of boxes lined up against the walls. Her room was almost bare. She was looking for other things to put in the open box, when she found a wooden cigar box under her bed that she'd been keeping her secret things in. She opened it and looked through it. She found some beer bottle tops from a party she went to with some friends from school, she found a small piece of wrapping paper from a gift she got from a boy she liked in grade school. She had a few pictures of her and Jason that she had forgotten about. Then she opened a letter that he had given to her. It was one of the letters he had written after the night at the beach. She thought back to that day. She started to feel the excitement that she had felt, when she was driving up to the house to meet Jason. She remembered the drive to the beach and how nervous she was. *Oh if only I could go back to that night, if I could just have a "do-over" maybe things wouldn't be so bad. Maybe Jason and I could have the relationship that we had always talked about, instead of a whirlwind romance, cut short by circumstances that were premature.* Christine thought about she and Jason getting married and having children the way it was supposed to be. *What if I would have said "Yes" the day in the park, when he asked me to marry him, after I told him I was pregnant.* Christine put the letter down. She took the pictures and folded them up in the letter. She stood up and walked over to her desk. As she opened up one of the drawers, the baby kicked. She grabbed some matches out of the drawer and lit the letter and photos on fire. She place them in a ceramic bowl on top of her desk and watched them burn. "Up in flames," she whispered to herself.

Just then, Edward rushed into her room, "I smell smoke. Something is on fire... What's...?" he shouted in a panic.

Christine interrupted him. "Nothing Dad, it's fine," she said with a little chuckle.

Edward snapped, "Christine, don't be burning things in here. Do you know how dangerous that is? You could catch the house on fire you know."

"I know, it's fine, and I won't do it again." Christine just looked at the charrd ashes in the bowl. *That's over, I'm not bummin' out over this anymore,"* she thought to herself. She went over to the radio and turned it up a bit. What Becomes Of The Brokenhearted, by Jimmy Ruffin was playing. She finished loading the boxes in her room and laid down.

Finally it was the last week of school. There were all kinds of parties going on and the kids were all excited. Christine was walking down the hall to her locker. A few of the girls she didn't really like, walked past her towards their lockers. She could hear them talking.

"What happened to her?" one girl asked.

"I don't know, but she turned into a real snob. She doesn't have any friends anymore. She doesn't hang out with anyone at lunch or anything. It's like she's too cool for anyone," another girl said.

The third girl turned and looked at Christine. Christine could see her staring out of the corner of her eye. "What's with the big threads? I thought that her parents were rich, and she only wore like, designer threads. Maybe her old man lost his job or something and she has to flip burgers after school to help out," the third girl said as she laughed. Then they all started laughing.

Christine closed her locker and walked past the girls. She bumped one of them with her elbow as hard as she could as she passed them. "Oh, I'm sorry, did I bump you?" Christine asked with a snotty tone. "You know, even if you put the three of you together, you still couldn't make one whole decent person," she said as she kept walking.

Christine finished all of her finals, cleaned out her locker and went into the office. "Mrs. Brown, I need to get my papers to enroll into another school. My family and I are moving out of the area."

"Oh yes, your mother called the other day. I have everything you'll need. I'll go get the papers." Mrs. Brown went to the back room and got the package together for Christine. "Here you go, these are all papers you should need, and when you get to the new school, have them call us if they need anything else. Where are you moving to?" she asked.

"I don't know yet, my dad got a job transfer."

Christine turned to leave the office and there was Jane, standing there, with her mouth hanging open. "You're moving? Where, why, when?..." she fired questions at Christine.

"Oh my parents decided that it would be fun to sell the house and go somewhere new. Since it's just the three of us and all," Christine said.

"I know, but you'll be a senior next year, don't you want to graduate with all of your friends?" Jane asked.

"Yeah, but – well, I don't know. It's no biggie. Hey, Jane, I hate to cut you off, but I really have to go." She gave Jane a big hug and she ran out of the office. Christine drove straight home. She walked into the house and slammed the door.

"Hey! What was that for?" asked Priscilla.

"Oh, I feel really crummy. Jane asked me why we were moving and I had to lie to her. Then some girls were talking bad about me today. Ugh..." She sat down on the sofa. "I just wanted to smack them. Normally I just laugh when I hear someone talking about me, but this time it was different. I got really mad, and I couldn't do anything about it. I'm just glad that tomorrow is my last day. This is really getting hard, and I think that people are starting to look at me different. You heard Charlotte. I haven't see her in a long time, and she noticed that I've put on weight," Christine said.

"Not that much. Really, it's not that bad, you just feel like the whole world is looking at you. When we move, no one will know you, it won't matter. You'll be fine," Priscilla said.

Christine got up for her last day at school. She took her time getting ready. Her mother was in the kitchen packing the pots and pans. "Here's some bread, make a piece of toast and get the jelly out of the fridge. We are going to eat out tonight, and then we will finish the last minute packing. The movers will be here first thing tomorrow morning." Christine made her toast and started to walk out the door. "Have a good day," Priscilla yelled from the kitchen.

As Christine drove to school, she looked all around at the houses in her neighborhood. She thought to herself that this would be the last time she would ever drive to that school. Soon she would be in a whole different area. No friends, no sisters, no anything. She took a deep breath and drove into the school parking lot. There were cars with toilet paper on them and painted signs hanging on them. "Here's to the Class of 1967," some read, others just read "School's out time to party." Christine went to her classes like normal. When she went into her art room, her teacher had cupcakes and cookies on a table. Some of the kids were sitting on top of their desks and some were standing by the table eating. Others were looking at the art work that was stacked in the front of the room, looking for their projects to take home. Christine walked up to the front of the class to look for her work. Her teacher said, "Christine, I will really miss you. I hear that you're moving away this summer. I was hoping you'd be here next year so you could really delve into your creative side. I am just so impressed with your natural abilities, this being your first year in art and all. I really do hope you take me seriously and take some classes over the summer. You really show promise as an artist. You should travel and learn a lot of different techniques, through different cultures too."

"Yeah, I probably will take some kind of classes this summer. I'm not really sure though where we are moving to, but I'm sure there will be some kind of school I could take painting classes at," Christine said. One of the other kids in the class came over and interrupted their conversation, and the teacher walked away to help him.

Christine looked through the piles of art work. She found her paintings, but she kept looking through the rest of the kids' work. *Wow*, she thought to herself, *I AM better than a lot of these kids.* She smiled to herself and walked over to the table to get a drink. She made small talk with a few of the kids that were standing around. Then she just didn't feel like even trying to connect anymore, so she just listened to their conversation. She shared some courtesy laughs with them and pretended to be interested in what they were talking about. The bell rang, and the excited screams of summer freedom echoed through the halls. The majority of the kids were all laughing and running through the parking lot like a wild pack of animals. Christine just slowly walked out of the school, and across the parking lot for the last time.

There were kids honking their horns and music blasting out of several cars. Christine just kept walking. She put all of her papers from the other classes in the trash can by her car. Then she put her paintings in the back seat of her car. When she got home, she took the paintings into her dad's art room. He was packing some of his paintings. "Dad, could you put these with your paintings and wrap them together?" Christine asked.

"Sure. I have plenty of room in this box." He looked at her work. "These are very nice Christine. Your teacher was right, you do have potential."

"Thanks Dad," Christine said as she felt a little validation.

It was finally the big moving day. The movers were there bright and early. Priscilla was rushing around pointing at things she wanted them to move with extra care. Edward was outside pulling some large boxes out of the garage. "Do you need any help Dad?" Christine asked.

"No thanks sweetie. I've got it. You could go see if your mother needs any help," he said.

"She's busy bossing the movers around," she said with a chuckle. "Dad, I need to say good-bye to Jane. Do you think that would be okay? If I'm only gone for a little bit?" asked Christine.

"Are you sure you want to do that? I think that it is going to be a bit emotional for you Christine," Edward said.

"Yeah it will be for sure, but I'll be fine. She was my best friend, and I just cut her off – along with everyone else – when this happened. I think I owe her that much," Christine said.

Christine slowly walked over to Jane's house. She wanted to give her one of her small paintings that she had painted of Jane and her dog. It was one of the first ones that Christine painted that she really thought was pretty good. She painted it the day after she met Jane. As she walked up to the front door, Jane's mother was walking out.

"Hi Christine, I haven't seen you around here in a long time. How have you been? What brings you over here so bright and early this morning?" Jane's mother asked.

"I know. It's been kind of a chaotic year. With Jane so busy this year, and my schedule... we just kind of lost touch. I wanted to come over here and see Jane one last time. My parents and I are actually moving today. I wanted to give her a painting of mine... something to remember me by. Is she here?" Christine asked.

"Oh I'm sorry sweetie. Her father took her to the beach house yesterday after she got home from school. I am leaving right now to meet them there. I had to work all day yesterday, and I was too tired to drive last night. I will tell her you came by though." She reached her hand out to take the painting from Christine. "I'll take that with me to the beach house. I know Jane would love to have it

with her there." Jane's mother looked at the painting. "You painted this Christine?" she asked.

"Yes Ma'am. I painted it the day after I met Jane. She was walking Rusty by my house, and I was washing my mothers' car. Jane
started a conversation with me, and we have been best
friends ever since," Christine said.

"Wow, this is really good, Christine. You should become an artist. I know that Jane will absolutely love this. Do you have a phone
number where you are moving to yet, so she can call you?" she
asked.

"No, not yet." Christine was holding back her tears. "Can you
please just tell her that I will call her, and send her my new address
as soon as we get settled? Tell her that I'm sorry I didn't get a
chance to say good-bye?"

"Sure thing sweetie. You take care of yourself, and I hope you
enjoy your new home." Jane's mother gave Christine a big hug
good-bye. "We will miss you Christine." She grabbed her bags from
inside the front door, closed the door and locked the deadbolt with
her keys. As she walked over to her car to get in she said, "Oh, and
don't be a stranger. Stop by whenever you are in town." She loaded
her bags, and the painting into the car, got in and drove away.

Even though she wanted to say good-bye to Jane in person,
Christine felt a bit relieved. It was better this way. She didn't have
to lie about what was really going on. With all the sudden changes in relationships, roller coaster emotions, and endless sense of
being lost in oblivion – Christine's carefree, happy-go-lucky days
were over.

When Christine got back home, she saw Charlotte, Peter, and
the kids walking into the house. They had brought a big lunch over,
and they were going to help clean the house after the movers were
done. They all sat around on the floor in the living room. They reminisced about all the fun they had in the house. All of the holidays,

the birthdays, the good times and the bad. They all laughed and ate. The kids went out into the backyard to play and the adults kept talking. Edward looked at his watch and said, "Well, it's about that time. I think we'd better hit the road, I don't want to get there too late. You know, mountain driving at night and all." He stood up and stretched. Everyone else stood up while Charlotte cleaned up the lunch plates.

"This is going to be a big change for you guys," Charlotte said.

"I think that it'll be a great change," said Peter.

Christine grabbed her mother's arm and pulled her into the kitchen. "WHERE are we moving to?" she snapped.

"Relax Christine, we didn't want to tell you because we didn't want to upset you. We are moving to Lake Arrowhead. It's a nice, quiet, small community. There won't be anything to worry about up there, plus the surroundings are so peaceful, I think that your father could really do some nice work up there. I think that the scenery will inspire him to paint again."

"Oh my gosh, are you kidding me? Do you know how far away from the real world that is? You expect me to live like a hobbit in the mountains for the rest of my life? This is totally not fair," Christine cried.

"It's temporary Christine. I mean..."

Just then Charlotte came into the kitchen. "Hey Christine, you'll have mom all to yourself from now on. Let me spend some time with her before you leave." Charlotte took her mothers' arm and they walked out of the room.

Edward and Peter walked through the house one last time, making sure that all of the boxes had been loaded and nothing had been forgotten. Christine walked out the sliding door to the patio. All of the patio furniture was gone, all the potted plants had been given away, and all the warm character had vanished, leaving a stark cement slab of coldness that seemed to echo much of the loss she felt internally. She walked across the patio, and past the pool. She went across the grass and over to a large oak tree on the far side of the yard. She hopped up on a wooden swing that her dad had tied onto one of the lower branches when she was a little girl. She swung as she watched her niece and nephews playing tag on the grass.

Charlotte came outside and called the kids into the house to say good-bye. Christine swung for a few more minutes, then she got up and walked over to the pool. She kicked off her flip-flops and stepped onto the first step and sat down on the side of the pool. She reached down to touch the water with her fingers. She moved her hand slowly back and forth, watching the little ripples of water float all the way across the pool. She thought to herself, *Kind of how life is. One little movement and the ripples just continue to grow.* She gazed deep into the water as if she was looking for her future to appear.

Edward came out of the house and saw Christine by the pool. "Are you ready to hit the road?" he asked.

"Sure Dad," she sighed. Edward put his hand out and Christine grabbed it and pulled herself up.

They walked through the house and out the front door. Edward locked up the house and then walked over to Peter, who was standing by Christine's car. "Here are the keys Peter. I really appreciate you storing this at your house for us while we are away," Edward said as he handed the keys to Peter.

Christine looked at her dad, shocked, her eyes wide with question. "I'm not going to get to take my car?" Christine asked as her voice cracked.

"No honey, Charlotte and Peter are going to keep it for us until we need it. I don't think that it's necessary to have the extra car up there right now," Edward said.

Christine stomped over to her fathers' car and she got in and slammed the door. "Wow, she's a bit moody today, don't you think?" Peter said to Charlotte.

"I don't think Christine knew she wasn't taking her car. That's not just 'moody' there's something else going on. I can feel it," said Charlotte.

They all said their good-byes and Christine's parents got into their car. As they drove down the street, Christine kept looking back at the house. She didn't notice the black Cadillac sitting on the other side of the street with cigarette smoke billowing out of the window. She looked back until she couldn't see their street anymore. Then she turned around, with tears in her eyes, and tears rolling down her cheeks, she knew that this was the beginning of the end.

CHAPTER NINE

It was early evening when they pulled up to the house. "Christine, wake up, we're here," Priscilla said.

"Ugh! I am so tired. I just fell asleep," Christine mumbled.

"Well, we need to make sure that the movers put all of the beds in the right rooms," Edward said.

"Come on Christine, grab the bags of sheets out of the back seat. Once we make the beds, you can go back to sleep," said Priscilla. They all walked into the house and looked around.

"How did you find this place?" Christine asked.

"I had a realtor looking around at properties for us, and she sent me the information along with some pictures," Edward said.

They continued to look around. The house was two stories. The main part of the house was on the upper level. There was a long stairway that went down to one large room. It had built in shelves from floor to ceiling on one wall. At one time, it had housed Keith Davis' movie memorabilia. There was also a half bathroom down there. It had sliding doors that went out to a very private and secluded backyard. The house had three bedrooms and two bathrooms on the main floor. It had a medium sized kitchen with a window that overlooked the woods and the lake. The house was very nice, which pleasantly surprised Priscilla. It was far nicer than she thought it would be. Christine went into one of the bedrooms. It had a beautiful view of the mountains on the other side of the lake, and it also had a small balcony. She opened the sliding doors and stepped out. She looked out at the mountains. She saw several squirrels running on the ground beneath her. She went back into the room, grabbed her sheets out of the bag and made her bed. All of the moving boxes were out in the living room. Christine went to get a few of hers, so she could make her room look more like home.

"Don't lift those Christine. I will bring them to your room in a little bit. I need to help your mother find the kitchen boxes first," Edward said. After they moved some of the boxes from room to room, Edward took Christine's boxes to her room. Christine was fast asleep in her bed with the sliding doors open and a gentle breeze blowing into the room.

The next few weeks were full of organizing and shopping for things that they needed. They all drove into town. There were all kinds of little specialty shops for tourists and Priscilla was excited to explore them all. Edward told Priscilla that she could do all the shopping she wanted, once they had the house set up. The people that they met, all seemed extremely friendly. After they did the last of the necessity shopping, Edward decided that it would be fun if they went down to the lake and to look around. It was a beautiful sight. It was so peaceful and quiet. Edward stopped the car and they all got out and walked around a bit. "This is really inspiring me. Nature always paints a pretty picture, don't you think." Christine looked at her father and rolled her eyes.

"I agree," Priscilla said. They stood there, admiring the lake for a few minutes, watched the birds soar overhead, and the other families enjoying their activities. Edward took a deep breath, put his hands on his stomach and said, "This is giving me quite an appetite."

"Me too, let's get the groceries home before they all spoil. We can come back and soak in the serenity later," Priscilla said.

They went back to the car and headed home. As they drove, Priscilla said, "Tomorrow we are going to see the doctor again, Christine. It's your last visit until you deliver. I wanted to get you in to see the doctor before you get too big, and people see us. You only have about a month and a half left, and you are really starting to show. We can't have you out in public too much from now on. We also need to meet with the social worker, and make sure that all of the forms and documents we sent them are all taken care of."

"Whatever," Christine said as they pulled up at the house. Christine jumped out of the car before Edward had even turned off the engine. She slammed the car door.

"Wow, she is really short tempered these days," Edward said.

"Her hormones are all out of whack, and I think that she's bored. Maybe you could get her interested in painting something with you Edward. Hopefully that could take her mind off of the situation," Priscilla said.

"That's a great idea Hun," Edward said.

They got out of the car, unloaded all of the groceries and Priscilla fixed lunch. Christine was sitting on her bed with the sliding glass door open. Edward walked towards her room and paused at the doorway. "This sure is a great view isn't it Christine? You know, I unpacked all of my paint supplies the other day. I thought that maybe I could bring an easel in here, and maybe you could paint something." Edward walked over to the sliding glass door, "Looking out from this balcony sure is a great picture. What do you think?" Edward asked.

"Sure Dad, bring the painting stuff in here, maybe I can amuse myself by painting... huh?" Christine said sarcastically.

"Christine, that's not fair, your mother and I are trying to make the best of this, and your attitude isn't helping us. You know, WE didn't just choose to bring you up here to live. This wasn't our doing," Edward said as he was trying to hold back his anger. "This whole situation..."

Just then Priscilla walked in and said, "Look you two, the situation is what it is. There's nothing we can do about it now, and thank God, it's almost over so we can all get on with our lives. Let's all just make an agreement. We need to get along. No more rude comments. Christine, no more snapping at us. We are all going to make the best of this. Understood?" Priscilla demanded. Christine just shook her head and rolled her eyes.

The next morning they all loaded up in the car and headed down the mountain. Edward didn't notice that parked in the driveway, four doors down, there was a black Cadillac. The same black Cadillac that Hushinson was driving when he met Edward in the parking lot at his office.

Mr. Hushinson had been monitoring the McMillan's activities. Wherever they went, he had been watching their every move. He had been reporting everything to Keith, who had rented the cabin for him to keep an eye on them. He slowly walked out of his cabin and got into his car. He followed them at a safe distance. They drove to Los Angeles, straight to the doctors' office. Christine went in for her check-up, while Edward and Priscilla had an appointment with the social worker, in the office next door. Hushinson pulled up outside the medical building. He waited for a few minutes before he entered the building.

Edward and Priscilla walked into the social workers office and signed in. A few minutes later, a dark-haired, matronly looking woman with a file folder in her arms came out of the side door. "Mr. and Mrs. McMillan, I am Mrs. Houston." She extended her hand to Edward and they shook hands. "Please come with me to my office," she said. They followed her down a short hallway to her office and sat down in front of her desk. She opened the file. "I will be handling Christine's adoption case. I received all of the paperwork to get going on the adoption. Since she is due in about a month or so, I really need to wrap this up. I know that there are a lot of suitable couples that are on the waiting list to adopt, so it shouldn't take much time to locate a home for the baby. I do need to meet with Christine and ask her some questions for the file."

"What do you mean, questions to put in the file,"Priscilla asked.

Edward chimed in, "We thought that this was all confidential. We don't want any information in those files that could link us to that child."

"Relax Mr. McMillan. It's strictly protocol. These are all non-identifying questions that we like to put in the files for the new parents to have. There is no way anyone will know anything. Trust me, we do this all the time. You are not the first people to come our way. Now, let me go see if the doctor is done with Christine." She smiled and walked out of the room.

"I don't know about this Edward," Priscilla said.

"Don't worry, I'm sure that we are just overreacting. I know I am. I mean, think about it, if we were buying a child, we would want to know something about it, where it came from, what kind of people it came from, you know, heritage stuff."

"They don't buy children... do they?"

"I don't think they just hand them out for free dear," Edward retorted. "That's not the point. The point I was making was that people are curious, and if they're investing in a child, that's a long term investment. They'd want to know as much as possible, don't you agree."

"I guess so," Priscilla said uneasily.

In the other room, Christine was finishing up with the doctor. "Everything looks good. It looks like you are doing a great job keeping the weight down. That will really help you after the delivery, you know, to get your shape back quickly. The baby's heartbeat sounds strong, that's good. Your blood pressure is fine. Well Christine, the next time I see you, you'll be delivering, and that should be in just about four to six weeks. Do you have any questions for me?" Dr. Newman asked.

"No, not really," Christine replied sorrowfully. The doctor looked at Christine puzzled.

"Are you sure you don't have any questions?" he asked again.

"Nothing you can help me with," Christine said.

He offered a sympathetic smile, squeezed her shoulder and walked out of the room. Mrs. Houston was waiting outside of the room for Christine. She knocked on the door and then she opened it. "Christine, I am Mrs. Houston. I am the social worker assigned to your case. Your parents are in my office next door. Can you come with me? I have a few questions I need to ask you for our files."

They walked over to her office and Christine sat down next to her mother. "We have some non-identifying questions to ask you that we pass along to the new parents. Your parent have filled almost all of it out. Let me see here – Christine, why don't you finish this side of the form where the missing answers are." Christine grabbed the papers and started writing. She handed the finished forms back to Mrs. Houston. Mrs. Houston read the questions out loud with the answers. "Okay, it says here Christine, you're five foot six, and you have blonde hair and blue eyes, and that you are seventeen. So you are a senior in high school next year, right?" Christine nodded. "Hum... she read down further. Oh yes, you have two sisters who are artists, let me see, that would make them 'aunts' to the baby. She wrote some notes on the form. Your father is an artist as well. This child could turn out to be an artist too." Christine's eyes started to fill up with tears.

Priscilla looked over at Christine and noticed that she was upset so she put her hand on top of Christine's hand.

"Well, I think that's about it for you, now, what about the father?" she asked. It was dead silent in the room. Edward looked at Priscilla who was looking at Christine, and Christine was just staring at Mrs. Houston. Christine moved her hand away from her mothers' and folded her arms. She sighed in annoyance.

She paused for a few seconds and replied, "He is nineteen years old, he has brown hair and blue-green eyes. He's about five foot ten I guess. He asked me to marry him and I said no. That's all I can remember about him," Christine blurted out.

"Okay, well, I guess that will have to do then," Mrs. Houston said.

"Can we go now?" Christine snapped.

Mrs. Houston looked at the file, glanced up at Christine and said, "Sure sweetie, you are done here." Christine abruptly stood up and started to walk to the door. Mrs. Houston got up from her desk quickly and walked towards Christine. She touched Christine's arm. "I know that you are going through a lot, and this isn't easy. You have to know that you are doing the right thing," she said.

Christine snapped, "Yeah, I keep hearing that," and she walked out of the room.

Edward apologized for Christine's rudeness and Priscilla tried to catch up with Christine.

"Christine wait right there for us. You can not go running off every time you get mad," Priscilla barked. She tried to compose herself. "Christine, we all just want what's best for you, you have to understand that," Priscilla said.

"Understand? Understand? That's all I hear, that I have to understand. Why the hell don't you understand? Huh? You know, I didn't get into this mess by myself, yet, I seem to be the only one who is dealing with this. Jason gets to go on and lead a wonderful life and never has to 'understand' what I am going through. The fact that he just completely bailed on me, and left me to deal with this, is too much. He promised me that he'd be by my side. He told me that he'd marry me. Maybe I should have said yes. Then I wouldn't be ALONE!" Christine started to cry. The elevator opened and they got in.

Over by the pay phone around the corner from the elevator, stood Hushinson. He was holding a newspaper up in front of his face. He heard the whole conversation. After the McMillan's had left the building, Hushinson left as well.

Hushinson went back to his office and called Mr. Davis. Erin was upstairs, walking past the phone as it rang, so she yelled, "I'll get it." She answered the phone.

"Hello, is Mr. Davis in?" he asked.

Erin replied, "Just a moment, may I tell him who's calling?"

"This is Mr. Hushinson," he said.

Erin went down the stairs and into the study. "Keith, there is a Mr. Hushinson on the phone for you. Are you in, or should I take a message for you," she asked.

"No, no, Hun, I'll take it," Keith said arrogantly. He put his heels up on the desk. "That is the man that's making all of our problems disappear," he said to her as he smiled. He picked up the phone and said, "Hush, my good man, Keith here, are the accommodations suitable for you? I hope that you have a good view of the neighbors," he said as a chuckle came from his overly confident voice. "So what's the good news?" he asked, as Erin walked out of the room and closed the doors behind her.

She walked up the stairs, picked up phone and instead of hanging it up, she covered the mouthpiece with one hand, held the phone up to her ear and listened to the men talk.

"I have been following them as you requested. They haven't talked to anyone, and they haven't had anyone up to the cabin. I do have a very good view of them and I have a lot of equipment set up to watch them when I'm not around. They have no idea that I am there," Hushinson said.

"Good, good, that's why I hired you," Keith said.

"The reason that I am calling, is that I followed them today. They took the girl to a doctor and spoke to some social worker person. I think it was a routine visit. They haven't taken her to any doctor appointments since they moved up to the cabin, so I knew that some kind of check-up would be coming soon. The girl looks like she's near the end. They are delivering at the Good Samaritan Hospital in Los Angeles. The girl however, is a loose cannon. She is not happy about this entire set up. I believe that she might say something to Jason. I don't think that her parents are too sympathetic to her situation. I think that they hate you almost as much as you hate them. The girl sounds weak. If she is pushed any further, she just might blow the whistle, and I can't put the Hush on that," Hushinson said.

Keith took his feet off the desk and started rubbing his forehead. He was getting quite agitated. "I don't give a damn about the girls' emotional state. If she wasn't such a little slut, she wouldn't be in the situation. Just make sure that she follows through. You keep on them. Lean on Edward if you have to, threaten him. Tell him to keep his daughter on a leash. I don't care what you have to do. We are almost out of the woods, and I am not about to let some two-bit tramp ruin my life, I mean my son's life."

Erin's mouth dropped open with disbelief.

"You know what you have to do, if it comes down to it Hush – so do it," Keith demanded.

"Don't stress over it. I know what I'm doing. I'm just letting you know how delicate things are at the moment, and how important it is that – well, I need you to do something for me now. I need you to make sure that Jason is out of the picture. I mean, completely hidden. He's your son, and I don't want to interfere with that aspect, so I'm not going to tell you how to handle it. But I am stressing the fact that the girl can not have access to him. I trust you'll figure out how to nip that in the bud. These people however, I don't have a problem strong-arming," Hushinson said with a snicker. "But, if there is any way you can keep Jason out of the way, you know, unable to be contacted by that girl, it might defuse a potentially explosive encounter, if she should lose it, and call him.

"Okay, sure. I get what you're saying. I'm on it. Just keep me informed," Keith said, and he hung up the phone.

Erin just shook her head and hung up the other extension.

Christine and her parents headed back home from their appointment, completely unsuspecting that Hushinson had been there, and had reported back to Keith.

For the next few weeks, the tension was high. Priscilla and Edward would take little day trips and leave Christine at home. She felt like a prisoner. She couldn't go anywhere. Even for the Fourth of July firework display, she had to watch the fireworks from her room. They glistened on the water as they exploded. It was beautiful, but it was lonely. The only time that Christine was happy was when she was listening to 'The End' by the Doors, or listening to the The Rolling Stones and painting. Christine didn't realize how much she liked to paint. She could just get lost in her mind and out came a painting with depth, realism and character. From nature landscapes with trees, blue skies and clouds, to animals scurrying around in the forest. Her creative imagination became her strength and her therapy. *No one can take this away from me* she thought to herself.

Edward was impressed. He would take her paintings and hang them in the living room next to the fireplace. There were three so far. "Christine, I am so proud of you. These are really good. I can feel the story you are trying to tell. That is what separates painters from artists," he said.

"Thanks Dad, that really means a lot." Christine felt for a moment that her father still loved her, and that things were the way they used to be. She was at peace with her new-found freedom of expression, and she loved it.

The time was passing slowly for Christine and since her parents weren't really around much during the day all Christine had was her music and her paintings, and the life growing inside of her. She didn't have anyone to share anything with. Her belly was getting large and extremely uncomfortable. The baby would kick Christine more frequently than in the past. It seemed like the baby knew when she was upset. It would push and stretch more and more during those moments.

Christine had tried to distance herself from acknowledging the fact that a little person was growing inside her stomach. At times she had even flicked her stomach with her finger and thumb in annoyance, when the baby moved. Lately though, it was almost a comfort, feeling the baby move. She didn't feel quite so alone. She even started talking to the baby. One day while she was explaining her painting to her large tummy, the baby pushed its foot out to the side. The baby must have been stretching, and when Christine lifted up her shirt she saw a definite foot. She quickly lifted her hand to the spot and gently pushed in. She could feel the small foot. Then the baby put the other foot up against Christine's belly and pushed. Christine started laughing out loud. "Hey, what are you doing in there?" she asked. She kept her hand against the little feet. "Was I boring you all my painting talk?" she asked. "Oh I know, you are getting cramped in there aren't you? Well, I can't do anything about that. I have a strict diet that I have to abide by. I can't get all big and fat or anything, it would look bad for my parents," Christine said sarcastically.

The baby pulled it's feet away from Christine's hand. "I'm sorry, I wasn't yelling at you. It's just..." Christine rubbed her stomach, "I don't have any control over my life right now. You came along, and my whole world got turned upside down. I don't mean to take it out on you, I mean, I know you didn't ask to be here. I have been kind of mean to you through all of this, and I'm sorry. I think that I just didn't want to get too attached to you. I can't keep you," Christine started to cry. She stopped rubbing her stomach and started to paint again.

Just then she heard a knock at the front door. When she

opened it, there was a messenger standing there with a package. He said, "Hello Miss, I have a special delivery for Mr. Davis. Can you sign for it?"

At first the name didn't register with Christine. She shook her head and said, "No. I think you have the wrong address."

He looked at his papers, looked at the numbers on the side of the door, and said, "Nope, this is the right address. You don't know a Keith Davis?" he paused. "Uh, Miss?"

Christine almost fell over. She was in complete shock. Why on earth would someone be sending something to Keith at their house? Christine tried to compose herself and she answered, "No, I'm sorry I don't know that person. Someone must have written the wrong address on the package. I'm really sorry, I have to go, and she shut the door.

She stormed back into her room. She could feel her adrenaline rushing through her body. Her hands were shaking almost uncontrollably. She played back the conversation she had with her father, about how he found that house. She just stood there shaking her head. She said out loud, "They're all fucking liars! All of them. I can't believe this shit. This was Keith Davis's house!" How utterly disgusting the thought was, that her own parents concocted this entire scheme to get her out of town, and away from Jason. *Did that mean that Jason didn't know? That he wasn't really in agreement? What if Keith had told Jason that I never wanted to see HIM again. What if both of our parents were plotting against us this whole time, and we could have been together?* The thoughts just kept rushing through her mind.

"Christine, who are you talking to," Edward asked from the other room.

Christine hadn't realized that her parents had gotten home. They were unloading some groceries in the kitchen. Christine stormed into the kitchen and started yelling at her parents.

"No one, I was just talking to myself. Were you ever going to tell me that you got this house from Jason's dad? Or were you just going to keep lying to me? Exactly what kind of agreements did you all come up with, to keep me and Jason apart?"

Edward and Priscilla were stunned. "How did you – who told you...," Edward stuttered.

"A delivery came for Keith Davis today. At first I didn't put two and two together, but it didn't take me long to figure out just how low you would sink to protect yourselves. I am so devastated, knowing how easy it has been for you to lie to me all this time."

Christine just couldn't believe it. Looking at her parent's faces gave it all away. They both went almost pale in color, and Priscilla's eyes were wider than Christine had ever seen. Edward couldn't even make eye contact with her at all. *Guilty! Unbelievable* she thought.

"Christine, you don't know the whole story. Yes, this was Keith Davis' house, and the reason we didn't want to tell you is because we knew it would be a very sore subject for you. Yes, it's true. He wanted us out of town. But, it wasn't just to keep you and Jason apart. He was trying to be nice, knowing that all of us were being put in a tough situation, and the equal embarrassment for our families – having you walking around town just would have been too much controversy all the way around. I know you're thinking the worst but, it's just not the way you think it was," Edward said.

"Why should I believe you? You seem to be able to lie to me with such ease, how do I know you're telling me the truth about this. And why on earth would you accept anything from HIM? If I even believe anything you've just said to me, that is still a direct slap in my face, from not only your acceptance of his offer, but at how easily Jason just ditched me. Are you telling me that he knew about this too? That he was in agreement with all of you, just to get me out of town?" Christine stood there with her arms folded, tapping her foot on the ground and waiting for the next set of lies to come at her.

"Honestly honey, I don't know if Jason knew or not. This agreement was a simple answer to all of our problems, and we didn't really feel it was wrong to accept. After all, we are the ones being inconvenienced. It's the least he could do it pay for our troubles. I would assume Jason knew, because this house was a gift to us. They won't be able to use it any more," Edward quickly rattled off as if he had already had this story in his head.

Christine just stood there, shaking her head. "This is unbelievable. Whatever. I'll never know the truth, so just forget it. What did you guys get at the store? Anything good to eat? I'm tired of all this healthy junk you keep pushing down my throat," Christine said as she riffled through some of the grocery bags.

"Christine, we've been through this before. If you want to get back to your regular size after this is all over, you can't gain too much weight," Priscilla said. Christine grabbed a bag of chips and started to walk out of the room.

"Hey, where are you going with that?" Edward asked. "Didn't you just hear your mother?"

"Yeah, I heard her, but this is getting old. You don't let me go anywhere, you don't let me eat anything good, and you treat me like a criminal. Oh, and you LIE to me. You know, I think that I've been pretty passive through all of this. Everyone is planning out my life and I have no say in anything," Christine snapped as she threw the chips to Edward. "You two are so selfish," Christine screamed as she stormed out of the room.

She went downstairs and out into the backyard. She sat on a pine tree stump looking out at the lake. Pine trees and junipers lined the sides of the property, with sporadically place pines trees in the yard itself. The branches of the trees created a canopy that shaded the entire backyard, except for the occasional sun rays bouncing in as the branches swayed in the wind. The ground was mostly dirt covered, due to the large amounts of dry, brown pine needles. There were quite a few large boulders here and there. She could feel the baby shifting around as she sat down. "Come on, don't you start too," she said as she rubbed a hard spot in the front of her stomach. "Is that your butt?" she asked as she pressed down a little harder. The baby shifted again and the hard bump went away. Christine just sat there, staring out through the trees at the lake. She could see the boats pulling water skiers going up and down the lake. She wished that she could be the one out on the lake skiing, and someone else could be sitting there in her spot. She continued to sit there for a little while longer. Then she thought about a new painting that she wanted to start. She got up and went back inside.

"Christine, dinner is ready. I know that you were hungry, so I made dinner earlier tonight. Come in here and eat with us," Priscilla said.

"No, I'll take it in my room. I just thought of a painting that I wanted to start," Christine said as she grabbed her plate and walked back to her room.

It was a full moon that night. Christine started her new painting. It was of the moon glistening on the water. She painted the stars' reflection on the water. She painted a moonlit bank in the background with two silhouettes of lovers, lying on the bank. She painted for about two hours after dinner, and then turned in for the night. She drifted into a sound sleep and she started to dream. She was wading in the water up to her ankles. It was a warm evening and she was dragging her feet in the sand on the bank of the lake. The crickets were singing. She was wearing a calf-length white dress. She had one side of the skirt in her hand and she was waving it gently back and forth. She splashed the water with her toes. She stopped and stood still as she looked up at the moon.

She was admiring the different colors that surrounded the moon. It almost looked like there was a rainbow around it. Just then, she felt strong arms on her shoulders. She felt a gentle kiss on her neck. She turned around and it was Jason. "I am so sorry that I left you Christine. I have been looking all over for you. I asked everyone where you were. I even went to your sisters' house looking for you. No one knew where to find you. You mean the world to me and I told you that I'd always be here for you. Why did you run away from me?" Jason asked.

"I didn't run away from you, you deserted me," Christine said as she pushed his hands away from her.

Jason put his hands back up on Christine's shoulders, this time, she was facing him. He started shaking her. "You left me. YOU deserted me," Jason yelled as he continued to shake Christine. She started to lose her footing. She struggled to get away from him. He just kept yelling at her and shaking her. Just as she broke free from his grip, she lost her footing and fell backwards, splashing into the water.

Christine woke up in a panic. She sat straight up and realized that her bed was all wet. The sudden panic continued to rush over her. *"My water must have broken,"* she thought as she started to cry. She rushed into her parents' bedroom. "Mom! Dad!" she yelled.

"What is it, Christine?" Priscilla asked.

"My water must have broken," she cried.

Edward quickly got up. "Okay, don't worry, it's going to be okay. I'll get her bag and go start the car. Priscilla, you get a blanket and her pillow. You should sit in the back seat with Christine and help keep her comfortable."

Priscilla helped Christine get dressed. They all walked out of the house and got into the car. Edward drove as quickly as he could down the mountain, and Priscilla rubbed Christine's head. When they got onto the freeway, it was much easier driving. Edward drove as fast as he could, as Christine let out loud cries from the pain.

CHAPTER TEN

Mr. Hushinson had a camera recording the McMillan's cabin. He had a small TV in his room that played the feed from the tape. It was almost sunrise. Mr. Hushinson had just awakened, when he glanced at the TV. He didn't see the porch lights on at the Mc-Millan's cabin, so he got up and looked out the window. The cabin was completely dark, including the porch lights they normally had on. There was usually a light on in the front room. He rewound the tape and saw Edward loading up the car. He watched Christine come out of the house with Priscilla helping her. He gathered up all of his camera equipment and loaded it into his car. He didn't need to rush out to follow them, he knew where they were going.

Edward was driving as fast as he could and they were almost to the hospital. Christine cried out as the contractions grew stronger. Priscilla just kept rubbing Christine's head and saying, "Breathe, you're going to be just fine."

Edward pulled up and parked the car at the entrance of the Good Samaritan Hospital. He checked Christine into the hospital while Priscilla helped Christine into the waiting room. When the nurse was done checking Christine in, she took her up to a room in a wheelchair.

Edward went back outside to park the car and then he headed up to the delivery room area.

The nurse was getting all of Christine's vital signs and gave her a gown to put on.

"Mom, can you please stay in here? I'm scared," Christine said. Priscilla helped Christine put the gown on and then helped her get into the bed.

"I am going to time your contractions Christine, then I will go call the doctor and let him know you are here. How far apart have the contractions been up until now?" asked the nurse.

"I don't know..." whimpered Christine.

The nurse turned and looked at Priscilla.

"Well I don't know either. I haven't really been paying much attention," Priscilla said.

The nurse just looked at Priscilla, then shook her head.

"Okay Christine, you're doing great. Just relax while I time them. It's important to know so that we'll have a better idea how long you have before you deliver. We need to get you sedated. Christine is your husband here?" asked the nurse.

Edward walked into the room just in time to hear the question, and quickly answered,

"Christine is not married."

"Oh, I see," the nurse said pretentiously. Her demeanor turned cold. "I'll be back shortly.

"I'll be right back honey," Edward told Priscilla and he quickly walked out the door.

"Excuse me," Edward called to the nurse. She didn't hear him so Edward walked faster towards the nurse, "Excuse me, ma'am?" The nurse turned around towards Edward, "I don't know where you get off acting like that to my daughter, you have no idea her circumstances, nor what our family has been through. I think that it is extremely unprofessional for you to respond to her in such a condescending tone like that just because you think less of her because she is not married. Do me a favor, don't come back. Send someone else who has some tact," Edward snapped as he stormed off back to the room.

Christine was whimpering through a contraction, and Priscilla was wiping her face with a cool, wet cloth. "How's my girl doing?" Edward asked as he walked back into the room.

"She's doing okay. Is the nurse getting the doctor?" Priscilla asked.

"I believe that they are calling the doctor and I requested a new nurse. One that isn't so opinionated," Edward said.

"Mom, this is really starting to hurt," Christine whimpered as she grabbed her stomach and her breathing grew more into a pant. "Oh my God, this is horrible," Christine moaned.

Just then, Dr. Newman came into the room. "How is everyone? I hear that your water broke Christine." He looked at her chart and rechecked her vital signs. "I just spoke with the nurse, and she said your contractions are a little less than three minutes apart. I know we usually sedate women, but unfortunately, we don't have enough time. You're going to have to do this without being sedated. I just need to speak to your parents for a second Christine, so just relax and don't tighten up your body. Just breath through the contractions. We'll be right back."

"Mom, don't leave me..." Christine said as she extended her arm to her mom.

"I'll just be outside the door. It will be okay Christine," Priscilla said.

They all walked out of the room. "I think that she is going to deliver pretty quickly which is odd for a first baby. Most people are in labor for many hours with their first child. Now, I know that Christine wants you to be in there for moral support, but I really feel it best that you just let the nurses coach her and guide her through this. I know we discussed allowing you to be in the room before, but I just think that under the circumstances – it's just better this way. I'll let you go in and tell her your good-bye's. I'll tell her that the hospital rules state you have to wait in the waiting room," Dr. Newman said.

Edward walked in first, followed by Priscilla and then the doctor. He said, "Christine, I don't want you to get upset, but the hospital rules won't allow your parents to be in the room when you give birth. I've asked them to come in and say good-bye for now so we can get you ready to deliver. You'll have plenty of support, so don't worry about that."

"We'll be right here the whole time Christine, just down the hall. They can come get us if you need anything," Priscilla said.

Edward put his arm around Priscilla and walked her out of the room. He turned while he was in the doorway and said, "You're almost through with this mess, and life can get back to normal. Buck up kiddo."

Christine just looked at them in disbelief. "What? You guys are going to leave me alone in here," Christine asked.

Priscilla poked her head back into the room."I know honey, but you heard the doctor say that it's hospital policy. We really want to be in here with you, but rules are rules," she said trying to stay calm.

Another contraction hit Christine. She was groaning and breathing a bit harder now. Her head was sparkling with perspiration. "Fine. Just go. Why should now be any different?" she cried.

Edward and Priscilla just turned and left to go wait in the waiting room.

Mr. Hushinson pulled up at the hospital. He drove through the parking lot looking for Edward's car. When he found the car he noted the location in his log book and then snapped a photograph of it for his records. He drove to a nearby coffee house where he saw a payphone outside and called Mr. Davis. The phone rang at the Davis house and Keith answered it. "Hello."

"Keith?" he asked.

"Yes this is Keith," he replied.

"Keith? Good. This is Hush. I have some news that I think will make your day. I followed the McMillan's this morning to the hospital. It seems that the girl is delivering. I noted that the car was parked in the parking, lot third row from the front, fifteen in from the left."

"I don't give a damn about where the car is parked Hush. The part I care about is that it's over. This is the best news I tell you. The best news. You have done an outstanding job," Keith said.

Erin was walking by the office when she heard Keith's overly excited voice. She quickly ran upstairs, into their room, and quietly picked up the phone.

"Do you want me to stay over there at the Good Samaritan Hospital until they release her," Mr. Hushinson asked.

"No, no that won't be necessary. I can handle it from here. I am sure that you want to go back up to the cabin, pack up all of your stuff and get the hell out of there. I know that you are probably glad that this job is done," Keith said.

"Well, that's my job. I'm happy that I could help you Keith. Let me know if you need anything else," Mr. Hushinson said.

"Will do, and I'll messenger over final payment today. Thanks again!" Keith said as he hung up the phone.

Erin hung up the other phone. She was was feeling very conflicted. Her love and loyalty to Keith had always been her top priority but the fact that she knew Jason had been completely left out of the loop, and was truly worried about Christine, and those thoughts tugged on her heart strings. Erin waited for Keith to leave the house and she decided to call Jason. "Jason, this is Erin," she said nervously.

"Oh hey Erin. Is everything okay?" he asked.

"Everything is fine Jason. Your dad went out for a little while, and I was wondering if you could stop by the house? I need to talk to you," Erin said.

"Sure, I was just heading out. I'll be by in a little bit," Jason said curiously. Erin paced through the house and looked around nervously. She heard Jason's car pull up so she walked over to the front door and opened it.

"Hey, Erin, what's going on?" Jason asked.

"Jason, come into the office," Erin said as she took his hand and led him. She closed the doors behind her. "Look Jason, I am in a very strange spot here. I need to tell you something, but I know that I really shouldn't. This is your dad's thing, and I shouldn't butt in. Do you remember when you and I talked before, and I told you that I wanted to help you," Erin asked.

Yes, I do," Jason replied.

"Look Jason, I don't want you to rush over there – I mean, seriously – I am just telling you this because I think that you have the right to know. I overheard your father on the phone this morning, and... well... Christine is at the hospital having the baby," Erin said in one breath.

"Oh my God, are you serious. I need to go," Jason said as he started to get excited.

"No Jason, you can't. At least not now. You have to wait until it's all over. I am sure that her parents are there and for all I know, that is where your father ran off to. You can NOT be seen there! Do you understand me?" Erin asked.

She began to feel guilty. She thought to herself how mad Keith would be at her, if Jason showed up there.

"Look Erin, you have no idea how much this means to me that you put your butt on the line to tell me this. No one has told me anything, and dad just buried the whole situation with me months ago. Like it never happened. I haven't heard anything about Christine or her family. I didn't know where they were or if she was even okay... or... if she was even still pregnant. For all I knew, her old man took her to get an abortion. I know I screwed up Erin. I know that I let my dad down, but I think that maybe you understand how I feel. I won't let anyone see me. I just need to see the baby for myself. At least one time," Jason said as he tried to keep himself composed.

"I understand completely Jason, trust me, but I still don't think that's the right decision. However, knowing you'll do what you feel best, if you need to talk, I'm here. They're at the Good Samaritan Hospital. But please, please keep this between us. I will deny ever having had this conversation with you if anyone finds out," Erin said as she touched Jason's arm. Jason agreed and he rushed out of the room.

Back at the hospital, Dr. Newman was in the room with Christine and she was breathing big, deep laboring breaths. "Christine, I told you to relax through these contractions. They are coming so quickly now we don't have any time to give you medication. If you're tense, it will take longer which means you'll be in this pain a lot longer. It is important that you focus and let your body respond to the baby," he said. The nurse wiped Christine's forehead. "Dr. Newman, I'm trying, but this is almost unbearable," Christine cried.

The nurse tried to comfort Christine, but Christine barely noticed.

"I feel like there is something wrong," Christine uttered as she let out a breath. "Christine, you're fine. Nurse, I'm going to check Christine to see how many centimeters she's dilated." The doctor positioned Christine's legs so he could check her. Her legs shook in the stirrups. "She's at nine centimeters nurse, I think that we need to get ready to deliver now. Bring the tray closer, and get ready to hand me the forceps."

Christine let out a horrifying cry. "Oh my God I feel like I need to push," she screamed.

"Christine, you can't push yet. You have to resist the urge. You're not dilated enough to push yet, you could damage your cervix." Dr. Newman pushed the nurse call button for another nurse to come help calm Christine.

The nurse rushed down the hall and into the room. Christine

was panting and crying. One of the nurses was holding her hand and showing her how to breath through the contraction. The other nurse was helping get everything set up for delivery.

One of the nurses told Christine that she needed to sit up bit and slide forward a little bit on the table, so she could adjust the bed.

"Are you crazy?" she cried. "How the hell am I supposed to do that?"

The nurse answered, "Honey, put your arm around my neck, now on the count of three, one, two, three." The other nurse came over to help them. The two nurses lifted her up and forward on the delivery bed and positioned her legs in the stirrups.

"Good girl. Now scoot your bottom close to the end," the nurse said.

"Good, that's good Christine," the other nurse said.

There was all kinds of commotion in the room. Christine was looking at all of the lights and then she looked at Dr. Newman who was walking towards her with his mask over his face.

"Here we go Christine, let me check you again and I think you'll be okay to push next contraction. Okay, get ready to push," doctor Newman said. Just as he finished saying push, Christine's body automatically started pushing. The nurse helped Christine sit up and grab her legs. They were shaking so violently from the stress she was under. Dr. Newman said, "Don't breathe, hold your breath and bear down, just keep pushing.

The nurse was counting out loud for her, eight, nine, ten. Okay, relax, you can breathe now."

Christine fell back on the bed. "Oh my God, how long is this going to take?" she asked. "I don't think I can take much more of... Aahh..." She screamed and sat up and started pushing again.

"Keep it up Christine, keep pushing, the baby's head is coming, and it's going to take a few good pushes."

Edward and Priscilla had just gone down to the cafeteria to get some coffee. When they got back to the waiting room Edward said, "Honey, I have a surprise for you. You have been so wonderful through all of this and since it's almost over I just have to tell you."

"Tell me what Edward?" Priscilla asked.

"Well, I have been keeping a secret from you for about a month, and I think that now is a good time to tell you. I called our old realtor Dolores. I had her look up some properties in a town not far from our old house. It is supposed to be a growing community, and it's going to be close enough to Charlotte, Peter and the kids, but far enough away from... you know..."

"What are you saying Edward?" Priscilla asked anxiously.

"I'm trying to tell you that I took some of the money Davis gave us and I bought you a new house," Edward said beamingly.

"Are you serious? We can come back and no one will know?" Priscilla asked.

"Yes. I paid cash, and I put it under a name they will never find. I'm not really that worried, we held up our part of the bargain, and it's not like the baby will be with us." Edward and Priscilla hugged and kissed.

"Thank you Edward. That IS a wonderful surprise," Priscilla said as a tear of joy ran down her cheek.

When Keith ran out of the house so quickly, he had gone to see his lawyer, Dan. "I got some good news today, and I thought that I should come and see you, you know, let you know in person. I need you to keep an eye on the adoption of this child for me. You know, just to make sure that it does go through. Hush did all that he could do, making sure that those people didn't talk. So far, so good. I'm just making sure that all the loose ends are wrapped up," Keith said.

"No problem Keith. I can monitor the adoption easily. Wow, this is great news for you," Dan said.

"Yes it is," exclaimed Keith. "Well, I just thought I'd stop by and give you the good news."

"Well, I'd say this calls for a drink to celebrate," Dan said, as he walked over to his bar.

"No, but thanks Dan. I need to be heading back to the house. I was in such a hurry this morning when I left, I forgot that Erin had plans for us to spend the day together with the boys by the pool. I had better get back before she has my head," chuckled Keith. They shook hands and Keith left.

Jason had gone back to his apartment. He sat there staring at the phone for about an hour before he got up the courage to call the hospital to see if Christine had delivered yet. The nurse who answered the phone told him that she hadn't, but to call back in a little while. Jason just paced around his living room. Thoughts raced through his mind about all of the fun that he and Christine had when they were together. He hadn't really gotten over her and since he had thrown himself into school and work, he hadn't even allowed himself time to process it all. It all came flooding over him now that he knew the truth. Jason was heartbroken, and the thought that Christine was about to give birth to his child, alone – without him, was pure torture. Jason started to get angry with himself. *If only I wasn't such a pushover*, he thought to himself. He walked over to a picture of his father and him. He picked it up and looked at it. "Why do you have to be such an asshole," he screamed as he threw the picture against the wall. He picked up the sofa and tossed it on it's back. His adrenaline was flooding through him so fast that it finally overtook him. He slammed his fist down on the glass coffee table and cracked into several pieces. Jason was yelling, "Why... Why did this happen... God this isn't fair!" Slowly stepping backwards, sobbing and shaking his head, until he backed up against the wall. He slid his back down the wall, until he was sitting on the ground. Jason hung his head down. He just shook his head in such disgust at himself. He should have stood up and been a man. He could have made it with Christine. They could have gotten married and had a wonderful life together. But instead, he cowered down to his father and lost the one and only love he would ever find. Jason looked over at the broken table and then noticed drops of blood on the carpet. His eyes followed the blood drips until they stopped at his feet. He lifted up his hand and turned it over to the side. That's when he noticed that his hand was bleeding. He went into the kitchen and washed off his hand. The cut was quite long, and quite deep. He tried to put some bandages and tape on it, but it was bleeding profusely. He put some ice in a bowl and then set his hand down in it. "Damn, this hurts like a son of a bitch," he said out loud. Then a thought came to him. He wrapped his hand in a towel and then taped the towel tight. He got his car keys and he ran out the door.

"Bear down Christine, it's almost here, I see the head," Dr. Newman said. Christine was tired and just about to give up. The nurse was talking to her quietly in her ear. Everything was almost in slow motion. Christine was pushing, crying, and praying. She could hear a faint echo of the nurse saying,"Push," in her ear. Everything was in slow motion. She could see Dr. Newman's eyes. His mask covered the rest of his face, but his eyes showed excitement. He grabbed the baby's head with the forceps. "The head's out, gentle on the push. One shoulder, the other shoulder. Okay Christine this is it. One last push," Dr. Newman said.

Christine gathered up her strength one last time. "Uggh," she pushed and let out all of her breath. "It's a girl," said Dr. Newman. The baby let out a loud cry. Christine lost it, her own tears started flowing uncontrollably.

After the doctor cut the umbilical cord the nurse took the baby girl to clean her up. "You did a good job Christine, she's beautiful," said Dr. Newman. Christine just laid on the delivery table, motionless as tears rolled down her face. The baby cried as the nurse took her out of the room.

"I'll go get your parents now if you'd like me to, Christine," said the nurse.

"No, not right now please," Christine said as she tried to hide her tears. The nurse grabbed some tissues and handed them to Christine.

Dr. Newman took off his mask and pulled off his gloves. "I'll come check in on you later, after you get to your room Christine. You did a great job. Try to get some rest now," he said. Christine just stared at the wall.

Dr. Newman walked out of the delivery room, towards the waiting room. Edward and Priscilla stood up. "Christine did a good job. The nurses are cleaning the baby up in the nursery. Christine needs to rest a bit, then you can go see her. I'll have one of the nurses come get you when she's in her room."

"Thank you Doctor," Edward said as he extended his hand.

"You are quite welcome," Dr. Newman said as he shook Edward's hand and walked away.

"So back to the house Edward. Tell me more about the house," Priscilla said. Edward told her that the house was in Westlake Village and it had a lovely yard. He told her again that he had bought it a month ago, and Charlotte had been decorating it to surprise her. They walked back to their seats in the waiting room and Edward kept talking about the new house.

Christine was resting in her new room. She was emotionless. The nurses couldn't get her to eat anything, or drink anything. "Christine, you need to get your strength back. You have been through quite and ordeal." Christine just stared at the wall in front of her. "Okay, well, I'll just let you rest, but I'll be back in a bit to check up on you," the nurse said and she walked out of the room.

Just as she closed the door, Edward and Priscilla walked around the corner. "Is that Christine's room,"Priscilla asked.

"Yes it is. I can't get her to eat or to drink. Maybe you can," the nurse said and she gave a sympathetic smile.

Edward and Priscilla walked into the room. "Hi sweetie," Priscilla said. Christine didn't answer.

"Christine, the doctor said that you are doing great," Edward said. Still nothing from Christine.

Edward and Priscilla looked at each other puzzled. Priscilla walked over to her and put her hand on Christine's and said, "Christine, Honey..."

Christine pulled away from her mother's hand, rolled over with her back toward her parents and said, "Don't call me Christine. It's Chris."

CHAPTER ELEVEN

Priscilla and Edward left Christine at the hospital and went to get something to eat. Christine was mentally off in her own little world. She was depressed and had tremendous feelings of guilt. As she laid in her bed staring at the wall, a nurse came in her room. She was a sweet looking, grandmotherly type. She had solid gray hair, light brown eyes and round cheeks.

"Hello Christine, my name is Dolly. I'll be your adoption counselor. Is there anything I can get for you?" she asked.

"No, and can you please call me Chris?" Christine muttered pathetically.

"If you don't mind me saying, I have seen a lot of girls in your situation come and go through this hospital. I know you must be feeling alone, but dear, let me tell you, you aren't the first girl to get herself into this kind of trouble, and you won't be the last." Dolly straightened the covers on Christine's bed. She sat down in a chair next to the bed. "You have to look at your life as it is right now, and what you have to offer a child today. You are still a child yourself. I know that you don't want to hear that, no one does. I think that the decision you made to give your baby to a family that really wants a child is wonderful," Dolly said as she was trying to read Christine's face.

Christine looked over at Dolly. She had such a sweet, understanding face. Christine felt very much at ease looking at her. "You know Dolly, in the beginning, I thought that I would be able to keep her. Then my parents said that I couldn't. I started hating the baby. I didn't talk to her, when she would kick or move. I ignored her and sometimes I would even flick my stomach when she kicked me. Then towards the end, it was like she knew that I was unhappy. When I got really upset, she seemed to move more as if to say, "I'm here for you." I started talking to her and rubbing her." Christine started to cry. "I don't care what my parents say. I want to keep her. I think that I am capable of raising her," Christine said.

Down the hall in the nursery, was the baby girl. All alone, no name tag, and no adoring family members gazing upon her. A nurse occasionally fixed her blanket, changed her diaper or gave her a bottle. She laid there, in her first hours of life with no one to bond to. All alone. One of the nurses walked by the baby and noticed that she had wiggled out of her blanket again. She picked up the tiny little girl and re-wrapped the blanket. "There you go little one. Why do you keep crying, we are taking good care of you," she said as she laid the baby back down.

One of the other nurses came over to the bassinet and said, "We are waiting for the social worker to come check up on the baby. She is calling the foster family to come and pick the baby up tomorrow, but she said that she wanted to come check on the baby today, herself."

"Oh, this always makes me so sad. Just look at her, lying there with no one to hold her. It's just so sad," said the first nurse.

"I know, but we see it more and more these days. Try not to let it get to you," said the second nurse as she patted the little baby girl and walked away.

Meanwhile, Jason had driven himself to the same hospital that Christine delivered at, to get his hand stitched up. He figured that if he could just get into the hospital, it wouldn't matter what time they released him, he was there, and could easily go upstairs to the nursery. He pulled into a parking spot, and turned the car off. When he went to pull his keys out of the ignition, he fumbled with them in his hand and then he accidentally dropped them next to the passenger seat. He was digging around under the seat looking for them when he felt an envelope. It had a heart drawn on the back, over the sealed flap. He gently slid his finger through the glued edges, trying not to tear it. Inside there were two pieces of folded paper. One was a hand drawn picture of the silhouettes of a man and woman. They were facing each other in an embrace, with two sets of flames surrounding them. One set of flames was a bluish color, and the other was a light pink. They were softly drawn, almost as if to show the energy between the two lovers. The other page was a poem. Jason was confused on how it got there. Christine must have dropped it the day she found out she was pregnant, when he had picked her up and took her to the park, or she had left it there for him to find as a surprise. He began to read.

"Hopeful Romantic — Moments"

My heart starts pounding, as you walk closer to me,
I've dreamt of this moment, for an eternity.

Wanting you to hold me, kiss me so deep,
As the moment grows closer, is this real or just another fantasy.

As you take my hand, and pull me closer to you,
It's a feeling I've felt before, even though it's all new.

It's as if we've already been here, in this moment in time,
I remember your heartbeat, as it melts mine.

Just for a moment, this crazy world doesn't exist,
I get lost in your eyes, and your deep passionate kiss.

Run your fingers, gently down my spine,
Hold me closer, and say that you're mine.

Passion takes over, building the heat,
Erotic shivers consume us, from our head to our feet.

It's just you and me baby, in this precious moment in time,
Soon this moment will be over, and the memory will only exist in my
mind.

His eyes filled up with tears, and he had a huge lump in his throat. He gently folded the papers back up, slid them back into the envelope and put it in his glove-box. Now, he was even more sure what he was going to do.

When he walked out of the emergency room with his hand all bandaged up, he headed for the elevator. He went up to the maternity ward. When he got off of the elevator, he could feel his heart pounding all the way into his feet. His palms started sweating. He cautiously looked down the hall to see if anyone was standing in front of the babies. He slowly walked down the hall, looking behind him every few steps. As he got closer to the babies, he could hear a few of them crying. His heart was pounding so hard he thought it was going to leap out of his throat. He looked behind him, and no one was there. He walked up to the window and saw a nurse doing some paperwork in the corner of the room. There was another nurse changing a diaper on the other side of the room. He slowly looked at the tiny bassinets. All of them had a name tag – except one.

That baby was set aside from all the others. She was wrapped loosely in a little pink blanket. Jason's eyes welled up with tears. There, on the other side of the glass, was his daughter. A daughter that he would never get to hold. Never get to touch. She was so beautiful. She had Jason's dark hair, and his button nose. He stood there for a few minutes, but it felt like hours to him. The nurse that had been changing a diaper noticed Jason standing there. She walked over to the little girl and pointed to her. Then she motioned to Jason, asking if he wanted her to hold the baby up. Jason shook his head no. He put his hand up as if to say, "Just looking at the babies." The nurse smiled and started tending to one of the other babies.

Just then, Jason could hear Edward and Priscilla's voice from around the corner. He quickly turned and walked in the other direction. Jason was so full of emotion at that moment, he wasn't sure what he was doing. The only instinct he had, was to get out of there. He ducked into the waiting room and walked over to the window. He stood there, frozen, staring out of the window. Edward and Priscilla walked past the babies, walked past the waiting room and straight to Christine's room.

As they entered the room, Dolly looked up. She immediately felt the tension coming from Christine. She stood up and said, "Chris, we can talk later." She smiled at Priscilla and Edward and she left the room.

"You look really good... uh, Chris," Edward said. "Wow that new name is going to take some getting used to."

"Mom," Christine sheepishly uttered. "Did you and Dad see the baby?" she asked.

"Well... uh... no... no... we uh..." Priscilla stuttered.

"What! Do you mean you weren't even a little bit interested in seeing my baby? Do you even know what I had," Christine yelled, as her emotions took over.

"When the doctor came out, he told us that you did really good, and we were just really concerned about you. No one really told us about the baby," Edward said.

"Well did you ask anyone? Oh never mind. I had a little girl. Maybe if it isn't too much trouble you could stop by the nursery and see if she's okay. No one will tell me anything," Christine said.

Priscilla spoke up, "Sure honey, we'll check in on her. Now don't

get yourself all worked up. You really need your rest. You'll be leaving tomorrow, and we have a long drive ahead of us. Your father
and I are going to go stay at a hotel nearby, but we'll be back in the
morning. We'll call the nurses' station after we get there and we
check in, to give them our room number just in case you need to
get in touch with us tonight." She leaned over Christine and kissed
her on the forehead.

"You get some sleep honey. We'll be back soon," Edward said as
he patted Christine's foot. Christine rolled over and put her back
to them. Edward and Priscilla walked out of the room.

"What do you think Edward? She seems a little emotional to me,
she couldn't stop the adoption could she?" Priscilla asked nervously.

"No, she's a minor and the paperwork has already been com-
pleted, that is why they have you do it all in advance. I'm sure that
a lot of girls get all emotional after the delivery, and they
aren't thinking clearly. I do think that we should at least go look at
the baby, that way she won't completely hate us," Edward said.

As they were talking, Jason could hear them. They walked right
past the waiting room and didn't notice him. They walked over to
the nursery window. "That must be her, the one without a name,"
Priscilla said.

Jason walked closer to the door so he could hear them. They
stood there looking at their granddaughter. Neither one said
anything. The baby just laid there crying. The nurses were all busy
with the other babies. She flung her little arms around straight
out of the blanket. She was all red in the face from crying so hard.
Priscilla could feel tears welling up inside of her. "Come on Edward,
I can't look at her anymore. I think this was a bad idea," Priscilla
said.

"I know it's hard dear, but we told Christine that we would check in on her. Now we did. I know that it's hard seeing the baby, but it's not our problem. We took care of the problem, now we just need to help Christine heal, and forget this whole mess," Edward said as he put his arm around Priscilla.

"You're right Edward, and it's getting late. I'm tired of being here," Priscilla said as she shook off her emotions.

Jason waited until they walked away and then he came out of the waiting room. He couldn't believe that Edward and Priscilla were being so mean, so cold, so uncaring. Jason still had a huge knot in his throat. He stood there wondering what he should do. He walked back over to the nursery window and watched his daughter for a few minutes. As he stood there, he played back the night that he told his father. He remembered how angry he was and how disappointed he was with Jason. He thought again about how he had thrown himself in to his schooling and didn't let himself think about Christine or the baby. He felt an overwhelming sense of guilt for abandoning her. Especially after hearing how detached, and cold Edward and Priscilla were. His eyes started tearing up. He thought to himself, *how weak AM I? I loved this girl and if the timing were different, I would have married her and we would be a family now. Why should it really matter how young we are? I know that Christine loved me. I know that it could have worked out.* Jason's heart started beating faster. He could feel a warm excited feeling deep inside his stomach, rushing through his body. He started to walk towards Christine's room. He thought to himself, *This is it. Fuck it! It's now or never. I know she still loves, and we can make it!* He slowly reached up for her door. He started to push the door open a little bit and then he heard her sobbing. Christine was sitting up on the edge of her bed, her legs hanging down over the edge and her back was towards the door.

"Dear God, why...?" she sobbed. "How could this be happening to me? This is so unfair!" Her sobs grew louder. Jason pushed on the door a little harder and started to lift up his foot up to take a step forward. He opened his mouth to say her name, when she blurted out, "What an asshole! I hate him!" She turned towards her pillow, punched it and then fell over onto it. Jason's heart sunk. He didn't dare go in now. He thought for sure that she was talking about him. He slowly put his foot back on the floor, backed away and released the door slowly. He hung his head low and slowly walked towards the elevator. He was brokenhearted. He pushed the button on the elevator, waiting for it to open. He turned his head back towards the babies, then towards Christine's room, eyes full of tears. Bing. The elevator door opened. He turned back toward the elevator. A completely devastated and defeated Jason wiped away his tears as he got into the elevator. His back still towards the door, head held low, he just stood there motionless until the doors closed. The sound of the doors closing behind him startled him out of his trance, slightly jolting his body. He just shut his eyes tight and shook his head.

The next morning Dolly came in to see Christine. "Hi honey, how are you feeling this morning? Did you get some rest?" she asked.

Christine was barely awake. "This nurse kept coming in here last night checking me to make sure that I'm not bleeding too much and poking my stomach. It was annoying," Christine said.

Dolly laughed, "well she's just doing her job. You know yesterday we were talking when your parents came in, so we had to cut our conversation short. Do you still want to talk?" Dolly asked.

"Dolly, I've been thinking a lot and... well... I really do think I could have raised the baby. If my parents would only understand," Christine softly mumbled.

"We talked about this Chris," Dolly said as Christine interrupted her.

"I hate my dad, He's an asshole."

"Chris! You don't mean that. I'm sure that your parents are only doing what they think is best for you. This isn't an easy situation, and I hope that you can look at it from their point of view," Dolly said.

"What about my point of view?" Christine asked. "Oh, forget it, I know that no one thinks that I could be a good mother." Christine sat there looking down at her blanket. "You know Dolly, I just have one favor to ask you. Since you seem to be the only one who cares about me right now, you are the only one I can ask. Can I at least see my baby?" Christine asked. Dolly looked at Christine. She just stood there, looking deep into Christine's eyes. She could see the pain in her eyes.

There was something different about Christine, and Dolly just couldn't put her finger on it. She squinted her eyes a bit and then she turned and walked out of the room. Christine sat up a bit in her bed. She wondered if she offended Dolly. She was a bit con-fused, but she kept her eyes on fixated on the door. A few minutes later, Dolly walked in with the baby. The baby was crying and her little face was all red. Christine's eyes instantaneously filled up with tears. Dolly handed Christine her baby girl. "Oh my gosh, she is so tiny," Christine said. She gently kissed her daughter on the cheek. The little girl stopped crying. Christine lifted up her little hands and touched her delicate fingers. "Look at her little finger-nails. They are just so cute," she said. The baby looked at Chris-tine. She seemed so peaceful. "Oh my gosh, she has my blue eyes," Christine could barely see her through her tears. She blinked hard a few times to clear her eyes. Then she gently pulled the blanket away from the baby's legs and feet. Christine held her daughter's little foot in her hand. "Her legs are so small, and her feet, oh my gosh," Christine could not believe her eyes. Dolly just stood by the bed smiling at Christine.

"She is beautiful Chris," Dolly said.

Christine held the baby and looked at every inch of her. She just kept kissing her little face. "You are my little baby Jennifer," Christine said. The baby made little cooing noises that just melted Christine's heart. About a half an hour had passed, when Dolly looked down at her watch and said, "Chris, I need to take her back to the nursery now."

"I want to keep her Dolly. I love her," Christine said.

"I know you do sweetie, but we talked about this, it's the best thing for Jennifer. If you love her, you should want her to have a happy, full life with a family that can provide for her," Dolly said calmly.

Christine hesitated. She wanted to argue her point, but she knew that no one would understand.

"Dolly, could you please do me a favor? Could you write her name on a tag for me? I feel bad that she doesn't even have a name," Christine said.

"Sure honey," Dolly said. Dolly gently wrapped Jennifer back up in the blanket. She let Christine kiss her one more time and she took her back to the nursery. The moment Christine let go of the baby, Jennifer started crying again, which cut through Christine like knife. She could hear the baby crying as Dolly walked down the hall. The cries getting fainter and fainter until she couldn't hear them anymore. A sound that etched deep in Christine's mind.

Edward and Priscilla had checked out of their hotel bright and early in the morning. Edward was so excited to show Priscilla their new home, that he decided to surprise her and show her before they went back to the hospital to pick up Christine. They were driving back from the new house, feeling so happy. "Oh Edward I just can't believe you did this. I can hardly wait to move in," Priscilla said with excitement.

"Well you can thank Charlotte and Peter. They have really been doing all the hard work. The only thing we really need to do, is bring our clothes. We can just leave the furniture up at the cabin. I mean, we'll need that stuff up there anyway. Charlotte got a big kick out of shopping for all the furnishings. When I called her and told her about the surprise, boy, she just ran with it," Edward said.

Edward and Priscilla pulled up at the hospital. "I hope that Christine will be able to leave soon. Do you think that we should tell her about the new house now, or do you think we should just surprise her?" Priscilla asked.

"I think that it would be a bit much for her to handle right now Dear. Let's just wait until we get back to the cabin. We can't move in for a few more days anyway, so why tell her," Edward said.

Dr. Newman was just finishing his check-up visit with Christine. "You look great Kiddo. I think you're okay to go. Just remember not to lift anything heavy for a few weeks, and get plenty of rest. I'd like to see you in a month or so for a final check-up."

"Well what's the good word, Doctor?" Edward asked as he and Priscilla walked into the room.

"I think that she's doing rather well. I don't see the need to keep her here. I'm sure that she'd rest better in her own bed, without all the nurses poking at her every few hours," the doctor said as he winked at Christine.

"Oh that's great news," Priscilla said.

Just then Dolly came into the room. "Chris, I need to go over a few things with you. I just need to make sure you..."

"Uh... Edward, let's wait outside until the nurse is done," Priscilla said nervously.

They walked out of the room and stood in the hall. "What was that all about honey, that isn't even the nurse," Edward asked.

"I just felt uncomfortable," Priscilla said. "I didn't like the way she looked at us the other day. I felt like she was judging me or something. I can't put my finger on it, but I just don't like her."

Dolly continued. "As I was saying, if you have any signs of

depression..."

Christine interrupted her. "Dolly, you have been over this with me already."

"Yes, I guess you're right. I just worry about my girls when they leave. They have an added emotional toll, on top of the normal hormonal adjustments. I guess it's just my grandmotherly instincts. I guess I just really wanted to say good-bye to you. I know that you are going to be just fine. You made the right decision Chris. I have been a special counselor for the adoption department for many years, and almost all of you young girls have second thoughts. I was trained to help counsel you girls, and help you make peace with your decisions. I am always here, if you need to talk," Dolly said.

"Dolly, thanks for everything," Christine said, and she reached out to give her a hug.

"You are very welcome Chris. You know, I have a feeling about you. I know that you are going to be just fine. It will just take some time, but you'll make it through this," Dolly hugged Christine and then she left the room.

As Dolly walked past Edward and Priscilla she said, "Make sure that you wait for the nurse to take Christine out of here in the wheelchair. It's hospital policy."

Edward and Priscilla walked back into the room. "Is it okay to come in now," Edward asked.

Christine ignored him. She gathered some of the spray bottles and after-care instruction that one of the nurses had left on the table for her. She put them into a little plastic bag. She took a look around the room and sighed. "Well, I guess that's it," Christine said very softly. Priscilla tried to put her arm around Christine, but Christine shrugged it off.

A nurse walked in, pushing a wheelchair. "Christine?" she asked.

"No, my name is Chris."

"Oh, I'm sorry, the paperwork says Christine. Okay then, Chris, are you ready to go?" she asked.

"Yes, I guess I am."

As the nurse pushed her past the nursery window Christine grabbed the wheel of the wheelchair and stopped it. Edward and Priscilla were right behind her. Christine scanned the babies looking for her daughter. She saw her off to the side. Her name tag was not on her bassinet like Dolly had promised. She was crying hysterically and none of the nurses seemed to notice her. She stood up from the wheelchair, gently tapped the glass, and tried to make eye contact with the baby. A nurse walked over and lifted the baby up. As soon as the baby saw her, she stopped crying. Christine took one finger and gently tapped on the glass again. She put her finger up to her lips, and kissed it, and then put it back on the window. She looked at her baby, with a soft smile and a tear streaming down her cheek. She stood there staring at Jennifer for a few minutes, then she solemnly sat back down in the wheelchair. Edward and Priscilla didn't say a word, they just stood there with their backs to the babies.

Christine looked over at them, then she looked down and shook her head. At that moment, she felt even more alone than ever. Everyone had let her down. Everyone had lied to her. She began wheeling herself towards the elevators. The nurse quickly grabbed the handles and started pushing Christine again. Edward and Priscilla looked at each other with a little bit of fear in their eyes, as they followed the nurse to the elevator. She wheeled Christine inside, and as the door was shutting, baby Jennifer's cries echoed through the halls and pierced right back through Christine's core.

CHAPTER TWELVE

"Ron – Ron..." Karen said as she gently touched his arm and shook him. The echo of baby cries rang through Ron's head as he awoke to find his wife and son standing over him. Ryan was crying, and Karen was bouncing him on her hip trying to comfort him. "Ron, I have been trying to call your cellphone for hours."

"Oh, I must have left it in the car. What time is it?" he asked as he sat up and reorganized the papers from the file. There was another handwritten letter at the back of the file he hadn't read yet because he had fallen asleep. He took those pages, folded them up and put them in his pocket. He walked back into his father's office and closed the door in the wall.

Karen followed him. "It's 2:30 pm. I got worried because I couldn't reach you. I called the hospital and they said you hadn't been back yet, so I figured you were still here. What happened? Why is the office such a mess? And why is there a door there? I never noticed that before." Karen walked over to the desk, bent down and started to pick up some of the things Ron had thrown on the floor.

"Oh, it's a long story. I'll explain it all to you later. I sat down for a little bit to regroup before heading back to the hospital, but I guess I was so exhausted, I just passed out. Have you heard from the hospital? Did they get any more results back from the tests yet?" Ron asked while still trying to regain his composure.

"No, they said there was nothing new to report when I called, and that he's still in critical condition. I think you need to head back over there babe." Karen helped Ron straighten up the desk a little bit more, then they lock up the office and they left.

She followed him back to the hospital in her car. When Ron got to his dad's room, he hesitated before walking in. Karen looked at him strangely with a little frown of confusion.

"What's the matter? Go in there and let him know you're back."

"Hang on a second, let me get my bearings here." Ron wasn't really sure how to proceed, or what to say. There was just too much information floating around in his head to possibly make any rational sense out of it, in such a short time. "Hey Hun, can you give me a few minutes alone with him?" Ron asked.

"Sure babe, I'll take Ryan down to the cafeteria. We'll be back in a bit." She leaned in and kissed Ron. "I know this is hard for you babe, and I'm sorry. We'll be okay..." she said as she gently touched his shoulder and walked away.

Ron walked in and sat down next to his dad. The constant beeping of the heart monitor, was like a metronome ticking the time away. He took a deep breath and looked around the room. He imagined Christine sitting in her hospital room, and assumed she must have had the same empty, confused, heartbroken feelings as he was having now. Her life had changed forever too, in a hospital room. He reached into his pocket and pulled out the last pages of the letter his father had written and started to read.

Something had come over me, when I packed up my equipment and left the cabin. I knew the job was over, and it became clear to me in that one moment, as I replayed every single event in my mind, that I assisted in ruining several innocent lives. For the first time in my life, I let it in. I felt ashamed. Even though I was told I didn't need to go back to the hospital to witness the end, I did. Carefully hidden in the shadows, I watched a young man's turmoil between following his heart, or obeying his father's orders. I felt it personally, deep in my core, like nothing I had ever felt before. I witnessed two completely selfish people, concerned more about their new home purchase, than their daughters pain. I saw the transformation of a young girl, into a completely defeated wreck. I watched the family leave, and as the elevator door closed, I knew the secret was swept under the rug, just like all of the other secrets I aided in covering up.

I walked over to the nursery window and looked at the baby. The social worker was there, getting ready to take her away. She was crying so hard, it went right through me. For one moment, it almost seemed as though she could see me standing there and she stopped crying. Her eyes pierced right through me, as if she knew I was to blame. I felt even more ashamed. She turned her head and began crying again. I not only witnessed two families destroy the love between two youngsters and toss aside an innocent life, but I assisted in it. Their need to protect themselves, at the cost of the other lives, was something that just rattled me to my core.

I had recently married your mother, and we had just learned that we were expecting ourselves. I thought about my own unborn child, you, and how much your mother and I already loved you. Your mother and I were elated. I couldn't imagine having you ripped away from us, without any say. I realized at that moment what unconditional love was, and that hiding indiscretions isn't helping people learn to embrace the true essence of life. Love. The only way people learn and grow, is when they confront their mistakes head on. Personal responsibility and accountability is a trait that I saw fleeting. Knowing that people like me, can simply lie and alter history and create a false illusion for what? Selfishness? Entitlements? Ego? I saw clearly, that these are the direct actions and destruction of morals and ethics of life. But 'Universal Truth' can never be altered.

Your mother and I spent many years growing in spirituality. Not religion, but in learning to recognize the patterns of the universe. The signs that are a gift from the divine that we all have access to, at every moment, if our hearts are pure. Perception is subjective. Everyone perceives what they see, either through what they were taught, or what they know from their own divine connection to source – through their soul. Sifting through ones truth means recognizing how to heal, by shedding the layers of ego. Ego is what stands between what we perceive we are and our truth. Under-standing that, is path to enlightenment.

No matter how many lies are told, or how much deception there is, the truth will always remain. I made a decision at that moment, to dedicate my life to helping people find the truth, instead of covering it up. My newly recognized passion for truth, was knowing that the only way to bring about change, is through unconditional love for all, not for oneself. Where there is resistance, there is fear of truth. Where there is ignorance and or belligerence, there is an extreme fear of truth.

This my son, is my truth. It has surfaced as it always will, and I own it all. It is the reason I built our business, and did my best, to instill such high morals, ethics and character in everything we did. Hoping to bring back to the world, what so many are hell bent on destroying by being selfish. It was the reason I had no tolerance for deception, lies and secrets. In the long run, any actions taken that weren't rooted in truth, in love – true, selfless unconditional love – it will be exposed, one way or another, under 'Universal Truth'. This my son, is the key to life."

Ron folded up the letter and put it back in his pocket. It became clear to him at that moment, that the reason his father was hold-ing on, was until the truth was finally revealed. Ron reached for his father's hand and held it tightly. He sat silently, treasuring what he knew would be his last moments with him. He fought back the tears and in a soft gentle tone he said, "Dad, I found the red file. I now know the truth. I understand the path you took, for it was a lesson you needed to learn, in order to make me the man I am today. I will treasure you always, for I only knew the most warm-hearted, caring, kind and honest of souls in you. It doesn't matter to me how we get there, as long as we do, for I only know uncondi-tional love. The love you proudly taught me.

I will treasure these lessons from you, in finding the key of life, and continue sharing it with others, in the hopes that I too, can inspire them to learn the simple lessons that you have taught me. I appreciate the opportunity that you have given to me – through the reading of the file – to be able to mentally walk the road of your transformation with you. Just as it was – as you were living it – so that I too can understand, how it would have been, living a life that I have personally have never known. It's easy for me to see the fear behind the choices that were made. You taught me well, about the ego, and it's need to overpower and lead people away from their hearts truth. It causes complete selfishness, greed, and flames hatred and jealousy. It's the root of self destruction. I can see it clearly now, how actions that are not rooted in a pure heart, can take lives down a very dark and lonely path. I now have a better understanding and appreciation for the struggles others may face, and gladly welcome this new information as a tool to educate and empower them to retrace their roots back to the core of their existence.

I am so proud of you, and the man you became. I can't imagine living a life, so unattached to truth, or unconditional love, nor would I want to, but I understand it now. Thank you for raising me, to be the man I am today. To see life through the open eyes of love, and walk the path of truth. I will always love you Dad."

Just then there was a soft knock at the door. Ron wiped the tears away and turned around. A beautiful blonde woman with blue eyes was standing in the doorway. She had heard everything Ron had said. "Ron, I'm sorry to interrupt... would it be ok if I came in?" she asked.

"Uh... yeah. It's ok, come on in," he said curiously.

"I don't know if you know who I am or not, but I'm the one who found your father this morning." She was in her late fifties. She had a aurora of familiarity to Ron, but he couldn't quite place her.

"I've been friends with your parents for almost twenty years. I've been looking after your father and tidying up the house ever since your mother passed away."

"I'm sorry, I didn't know he had anyone coming to check in on him. This is all new news to me. The hospital said that the house-keeper found him, and it puzzled me, but there was so much com-motion going on, I didn't even stop to question it. I'm sorry, I am trying to process so much... I'm just..." Ron stuttered.

"I usually check in on him in the evenings. Sometimes I bring dinner over, and other times we go out to eat. We made it a habit to get together a few times a week. When your mother was alive, they'd come to my house and we'd have dinner and watch the sun set from the patio. Your parents were my saving grace. They found me at a really rough time in my life, and they helped guide me back to my path." She walked over to the opposite side of Robert, pulled up a chair and sat down.

Ron was intrigued with her story. He watched as she gazed lovingly at Robert.

"Your parents helped me start an art studio. They funded the entire thing. I've been teaching art classes for about fifteen years now. We decided together that a beautiful way to show others about truth in compassion, would be if I could give back to the community by offering some classes for free to struggling teens. They could come learn how to express themselves on canvas as a healing tool. When I started offering the free classes, it seemed that my paying customers grew in tremendous numbers. It was like the Universe was rewarding me for simply doing something I was passionate about. It was through those kinds of divine interven-tions – that your parents helped guide me to see – that there is a much deeper connection with this life, than what we're taught. When your mother passed away, I asked your father if I could dedi-cate a special meditation room to her. She is the one who taught me how to meditate, so I wanted to honor her by creating a special room that would further help others find their inner peace. I have a beautiful, etched, stained glass piece, hanging above the door to the meditation room honoring her. It's the *Grace room*."

Ron could feel his heart expanding for his parents. He thought he knew everything about them, but this was a whole new level.

"Your dad always said, *Show them your actions, not your words.*"

Ron laughed and chimed in and they both said, *"Words are empty and full of ego."*

"Wow, this is blowing me away right now. I am mesmerized to hear someone else say the same things he said and showed me. This is absolutely divine energy pulsating through this room," he said.

"Yes, your parents were on a whole different level than most, but the most beautiful part was how they seemed to be able to meet people at the very level they were on. Watching them interact with people, completely unattached to judgment, control or force... just letting go of expectations... unconditional in it's finest. No words could ever match that feeling, which is when I understood why he came up with that saying."

"I feel exactly what you're saying. This is how I was raised, so I truly appreciate seeing the transformation through your eyes. It gives me a whole new level of understanding how we, as society, can be so blinded by perception – that our ego latched onto – in order to justify not wanting to step into the truth. You said they found you at a rough time in your life. Can you please tell me more about that?" he asked.

"Absolutely. Someone I cared deeply for once, died suddenly. It was a total shock to me. The papers said it was due to medical complications. Your father showed me the truth. It was a hard pill to swallow at the time, but that is the only way we understand the way back to ourselves. Robert found out that the true cause of death was a lie. He had a tumultuous life and never found his own inner strength. He let the anger towards others, control and consume his decisions, instead of learning to turn that anger into his own inner light. He was stuck in his own insecurities and ego attachments. Blaming the outside world, instead of seeing it as stepping stones to the path of freedom. He ultimately died of a suicide by overdose at a young age. I too, was locked in that negative pattern, and had your parents not come into my life when they did, I truly believe I wouldn't be here today. Your parents also showed me how to understand death. The attachments we have to others causes us pain when we lose someone. But, from witnessing certain things myself, I understand that once our purpose here is over, we simply go home."

"Wow, I'm so sorry to hear that," Ron said sympathetically. I know, it's not always easy for people to find out the truth, which is a difficult part of this business. But, like they say, it's better to be slapped with the truth, than kissed with a lie. It's hard for many people to accept that at first, but eventually they learn to acknowledge it."

She laughed. "I know liars all too well. I dealt with many over the years and how conniving they are when their own reputations and ego's are at stake. One of the first things your father helped me understand was one of the most poignant phrases that stuck with me. He said, 'Storms of desperation blow anger, fear, and lies as the truth of hypocrisy is illuminated. Only trees deeply rooted in universal truth will remain standing, among those who blindly rooted lightly in the soil of deceit.'

"He has many wonderful phrases. He says he didn't come up with them, they were gifted to him from the divine. Growing up the way I did, I guess it's hard for others to understand because they've been brainwashed by fear teachings. I'm not saying I don't have fear, and I don't get angry. Hell yeah I do. But, it's far easier for me to work through those energies and seeing how my parents guided others, like yourself, is just heartwarming to me," Ron said.

"Like I said, your parents were truly inspiring. When I came here today, I had no expectations. I felt pulled to come over, like the timing was right. Initially my thoughts were to just leave a note on your dad's desk and wait for you to find it, but that just didn't feel right. That was my own ego running the fear program again." She laughed. "It's a daily reality check isn't it?" she asked. Ron laughed back and nodding in agreement. "After sitting here and talking with you, I know too clearly I was following universal guidance to come."

She looked lovingly at Robert, and said, "Thank you."

Ron's curiosity peaked.

"When I found your dad, he was sitting at his desk. There was an envelope under his head, and a letter in his hand. I checked his pulse and couldn't find one. I gently laid him on the floor and called 9II. They told me how to perform CPR and I did that until the para-medics arrived. I was quite shaken and didn't remember the letter he was holding until much later. When I walked back over to his desk, I saw the letter on the floor. I picked it up and started read-ing it. Your father had been helping me find someone. We'd been looking since the day I met your parents. One dead end after the other. He told me to have faith. I would get so frustrated, then I would get angry, but he never faltered in his faith. He kept telling me that there is a divine timing and order in the Universe and the force of the ego blocks it. In the beginning, I just couldn't grasp that concept. It actually pissed me off when he'd say it. He'd just laugh and hug me. Those hugs meant the world to me. They kept me grounded. They gave me strength. Your mother was like an Angel. She had so much love inside of her. She treated me as if I was her own daughter. They were the parents I never had. The letter he was holding was the information we were waiting for. He found who I was looking for."

"Wow, this is absolutely incredible. I have goose bumps on my arms," Ron said rubbing them.

"When I came in, you were talking to your dad about a letter he had written you. I helped him with that file. I filled in all the missing pieces for him. In writing the entire thing to you, he got to experience everything, not only from his eyes, but through mine. I gave him just as much as he's given me. A deeper understanding about the spiritual journey to enlightenment. Until we can see life through each other eyes, we are only living half truth. I am Christine."

Ron's eyes filled up with tears. He just couldn't believe what he was hearing. He choked back the tears and asked, "The person you lost was Jason? That's when my parents found you?"

"Yes. That's when they saved me."

"So you found your daughter then too?"

Just then, Karen and Ryan walked into the room.

Christine stood up. Her heart started beating faster and her eyes filled up with joyous tears. "Yes," she cried. "She just walked in."

Robert's monitors flat-lined in one more divinely timed moment. The truth had set him free.

ABOUT ME, AND MY DIVINE
GUIDANCE TO WRITE THIS BOOK

In the midst of the chaos, we perceive as life, is the brilliant gift of coming home. This book was part of my personal journey of remembering that truth. All of the outside forces that I perceived to be against me, were in truth, puzzle pieces I gave to myself, prior to being born, to remind me of the truth. It was only through the remembrance of this, untangling the web of lies that my mind latched onto – as the false narrative of egoic control – and diving deep down the rabbit hole, was I able to start truly seeing the truth in the puzzle piece clues. The universe is truly a remarkable place, once we learn to detach from the shackles of earthly confines.

The events I thought defined me, were nothing but illusions the ego created to stay in control. But in truth, the illusions of control are the illusions of suffering. Micromanaging has been brainwashed into us as children. We were micromanaged from day one, and taught the false idea of "self" means to dominate, seek to control others, and focus on "outside" issues, in order to create an identity. Staying locked in a victim mentality is what keeps us from waking up, and coming home. Step by step, piece by piece, when we understand our path – our puzzle pieces – our perceptions shift, our sight becomes more and more clear, and we appreciate every single miraculous sign we are able to recognize. We begin to see, where we used to be, in others who haven't detached from the ego mind. That truth deepens our compassion, our integrity, and our love. Not through the ego need to micromanage. Everything is connected, and when our eyes are truly open, every single moment in the 'NOW' is absolutely magnificent. The key to unlocking the puzzle you created is remembering your truth, your universal truth. You have free will to tap back into your truth. You can live a false illusion as the little 'you', or you can choose to detach from that programming, and reclaim your truth of oneness with the big 'U'. The Universe.

I BELIEVE IN YOU

Dear inner child, you are safe and you are loved,
It's time to crawl out of that cage, and fly high up above,

I know you were wounded, denied your true bliss,
By deceived guiders who shamed you, but they too were amiss,

You were always so worthy, of taking your stand,
I am older and wiser now – guiding you, and holding your hand,

Together we now merge, back into one,
We are protected, and united, by Universal forces stronger than
the sun,

Release now the past, the shackles of lies,
We've been cleansed of our pains now, there is no truth in old
alibies,

Wipe off the tears, from your stained little face,
And stand tall with me now, full of trust and an abundance of faith,

Never were you forsaken, I know you're tired of the dark,
Those illusions were simply lessons, to reignite our inner spark.